T

The Pillars

Morris L. Venden

Pacific Press Publishing Association
Mountain View, California
Oshawa, Ontario

ISBN 0-8l63-0483-1

Contents

The Landmarks Defined

"In Minneapolis God gave precious gems of truth to His people in new settings. This light from heaven by some was rejected with all the stubbornness the Jews manifested in rejecting Christ, and there was much talk about standing by the old landmarks. But there was evidence they knew not what the old landmarks were. There was evidence and there was reasoning from the word that commended itself to the conscience; but the minds of men were fixed, sealed against the entrance of light, because they had decided it was a dangerous error removing the 'old landmarks' when it was not moving a peg of the old landmarks, but they had perverted ideas of what constituted the old landmarks.

"The passing of the time in 1844 was a period of great events, opening to our astonished eyes the cleansing of the sanctuary transpiring in heaven, and having decided relation to God's people upon the earth, [also] the first and second angels' messages and the third, unfurling the banner on which was inscribed, 'The commandments of God and the faith of Jesus.' One of the landmarks under this message was the temple of God, seen by His truth-loving people in heaven, and the ark containing the law of God. The light of the Sabbath of the fourth commandment flashed its strong rays in the pathway of the transgressors of God's law. The nonimmortality of the wicked is an old landmark. I can call to mind nothing more that can come under the head of the old landmarks. All this cry about changing the old landmarks is all imaginary.

"Now at the present time God designs a new and fresh impetus shall be given to His work. Satan sees this, and he is determined it shall be hindered. He knows that if he can deceive the people who claim to believe present truth, [and make them believe that] the work the Lord designs to do for His people is a removing of the old landmarks, something which they should, with most determined zeal, resist, then he exults over the deception he has led them to believe."— *Counsels to Writers and Editors*, pp. 30, 31.

The Pillars of the Faith

A man was approached by someone who asked, "Sir, could you tell me what you believe?"

The reply: "I believe what my church believes."

But the questioner was not satisfied. "Well," he said, "What is it that your church believes?"

The man thought for a moment, then said, "My church believes what I believe."

Not thus to be put off, the questioner then asked, "So what is it that you and your church believe?"

The man responded, "Why, we both believe the same thing."

If there were ever a time when that was not a good enough answer, it is today. There has to be a better answer for any Christian, and particularly for the Seventh-day Adventist Christian. Do you know what you believe? Do you know why you believe it? Are you familiar with the pillars of your faith?

Let's begin by looking briefly at the pillars of the Christian religion at large. There are certain monumental pillars, great truths of the Bible, that the Evangelicals have held. There are landmarks of the fundamentally orthodox, Bible-believing Christians that they have fought for, lived for, and died for. They are the essence of the Christian faith. And they are beliefs that we as Seventh-day Adventists share.

First, they believe in the inspiration of the Bible. They accept it as the Word of God and as the rule of faith and practice. They believe that "prophecy came not in old time by the will of man: but holy men of God spake as they were moved by the Holy Ghost." 2 Peter 1:21. They accept the Word of God as being "given by inspiration of God" and being "profitable for doctrine, for reproof, for correction, for instruction in righteousness." 2 Timothy 3:16.

Second, they believe in the Trinity. They accept the Three Persons of the Godhead as being all-knowing, all-powerful, and everywhere present—God the Father, God the Son, and God the Holy Spirit. They believe that God the Son was the Creator, was with God from the beginning of eternity, and *was* God. See John 1:1-3. They accept the truth that He possessed a divine, as well as a human, nature when He came to this earth to live and die for us.

Third, they believe in Creation. Of course, there are varying interpretations of the Creation story, but they still believe in Creation in one form or another.

Fourth, they believe in the fallen condition of man. They accept that "there is none righteous, no, not one." Romans 3:10.

Then comes the great truth of Christ's atonement for us. "Christ died for our sins according to the scriptures." 1 Corinthians 15:3. They believe in salvation by faith in Christ, not by works. The Christian religion is distinguished from the other world religions as being the only one which teaches that mankind cannot save himself—that he needs a Saviour.

Sixth, they believe in regeneration and sanctification by the Holy Spirit. They accept the words of Jesus to Nicodemus in John 3, "Except a man be born again, he cannot see the kingdom of God." "Except a man be born of water and of the Spirit, he cannot enter into the kingdom of God." Verses 3, 5.

Seventh, they believe in the spiritual unity and mission of the church, including stewardship.

And finally, they accept the sacraments of the Lord's Supper, baptism, and marriage.

We as Seventh-day Adventist Christians can identify with Christians everywhere in accepting and proclaiming these beliefs today. But do you as a Seventh-day Adventist understand what is unique and different about your beliefs? Do you know what distinguishes you from the rest of the Evangelical Christians? Do you know what beliefs you have that set you apart and give you a special mission to the world?

More and more people, particularly young people, are questioning whether being a Seventh-day Adventist Christian is really important. We have been invited to study and investigate the pillars of our faith, to understand their importance. One of our pioneers said in the last century, "If the pillars of our faith will not stand the test of investigation, it is time that we knew it." If that statement was true then, how much more true it is today, as we near the end of our opportunity to offer salvation to a dying world. Not only can the great pillars of our faith bear investigation, but as we study their significance, we will be given increased light and understanding; for "the path of the just is as the shining light, that shineth more and more unto the perfect day." Proverbs 4:18.

In the last century, when our pioneers had gotten the message that we were supposed to build on the foundation of justification by faith that Luther had laid, they began to build on that foundation the walls of santification by faith, including God's law and His

11

commandments in all their beauty. But as time passed, they began to take the foundation for granted. Finally they were told that they had preached the law until they were as dry as the hills of Gilboa, having neither dew nor rain. They were told that they needed to preach Christ in the law.

With this kind of encouragement, toward the end of the last century there came a rising emphasis on the theme of salvation by faith in Jesus Christ alone. Evidently there had been a vacuum, and people were eager for this truth. But as it was accepted with joy by some, others began to get nervous. They said, We've got to be careful. If we spend too much time on righteousness by faith in Christ, we'll forget our good old doctrines and the landmarks and pillars of our faith.

Evidently they wrote letters to headquarters expressing these views, and the nervousness continued to mount until there was a written reply which you can read today in *Counsels to Writers and Editors*, pages 30 and 31. To paraphrase, this is what they were told: These people are worried that the pillars of our faith are going under because of the emphasis on salvation by faith alone. But there is a misunderstanding of what the pillars even are! And then the author lists six pillars. The author concludes, These are the pillars of the faith—at least all the ones I can remember! But the author's point is that emphasis on salvation by faith alone is not going to do any damage to these pillars of our faith.

What were the pillars of our faith that were listed? Let's notice them briefly to begin with, to get an overview.

First, the investigative judgment and the sanctuary that brings this judgment to light. Second, the three angels' messages of Revelation 14. Third, the law of

God. Fourth, the faith of Jesus. Fifth, the Sabbath. And sixth, the state of the dead. We will also include as a sort of appendix a final pillar, the special gift to this church, which is the source of the list of the other six!

As we take each one of these pillars in the following chapters, we will notice first of all a little history, a brief outline of how each pillar came to be accepted by our church. We will also notice how each one of the pillars is inherent in the three angels' messages. And finally, we will take a long look at each one of these pillars to see how they fit together with the great theme of salvation through faith in Jesus Christ alone, in its twofold application. We will discover that the gospel of Christ, which includes both forgiveness for sin *and* power to obey, is the foundation for each of the pillars or landmarks of our faith.

Let's back up and consider these briefly, one by one.

1. The investigative judgment and the sanctuary that brings this judgment to light. Are you aware of the tremendous significance to us in the study of, and understanding of, the sanctuary and the investigative judgment? Or are you one of those second-, third-, or fourth-generation church members who years ago got fed up with the incense and smoke and rams' skins dyed red, and all the rest of it? I have experienced that, and it wasn't until only recently that the tremendous significance of the sanctuary and the investigative judgment has begun to come clear in my own mind.

Perhaps you are aware that the investigative judgment truth has come under the fire of Evangelicals. They have charged in the past that Adventists have held on to this doctrine merely to try and explain their disappointment, their mistake of 1844. They say that we misuse Scripture, connecting Daniel 8 and Leviticus 16, when, according to them, there is no connection betwen them. Are you familiar with the problem? Have you dealt with it? Are you interested? Let's study it together.

2. The three angels' messages. Have you ever, as a Seventh-day Adventist, thought that the primary message of the three angels was (a) prepare for the judgment, (b) watch out for Babylon, and (c) beware of the Beast? Or have you seen the thread running through each of these messages that is a warning against trying to save yourself and an invitation to come to Jesus and experience the deeper life of relationship with Him? If you haven't seen that yet, I invite you to study it carefully.

3. The law of God. What is the mission of the remnant people, who live at the very close of time, as it relates to the law of God? The last issue concerning the law of God is whether or not it can be kept. The real question in this pillar is whether or not the grace of God is sufficient to enable sinners to obey the commandments of God. And it is an extremely pertinent question for you as a Seventh-day Adventist.

4. The faith of Jesus. The faith of Jesus is our only hope for anything of value. If you check the original language, you will discover that this phrase (from Revelation 14:12) can be translated either "faith of Jesus" or "faith in Jesus." I'd like to suggest that both are correct—the reason that we can experience the faith of Jesus is that we have faith in Jesus.

As we consider the kind of faith that Jesus had, it is important to remember that faith, in its deepest meaning, includes the idea of trust. And when you talk about trust, you always have to have an object to trust. When we have the faith of Jesus, we will trust another, just as Jesus did. We won't depend upon our own strength or power or righteousness.

14

5. The Sabbath. What is the issue here? It's far more than just a day of worship. The Sabbath has always been a sign of sanctification. The Sabbath, according to Hebrews 4, is a sign of ceasing from our own works and entering into His rest. And the false sabbath accepted by Babylon becomes a symbol of man's trying to be God, man's own efforts toward salvation, man doing it himself.

6. The state of the dead. I don't like to call this the "dead" pillar—so we sometimes refer to it from the positive side as the "life in Christ pillar." Two of the most fascinating things you discover when you study the state of the dead is what Jesus has done for us and what He wants to do in us! How? Jesus' death at the cross, of course, reminds us of what He has done for us. But His resurrection reminds us of what He wants to do in us. Read this in Romans 6. We are buried with Him by baptism, that we should rise to—what?—walk in newness of life. Even here we see the twofold theme in salvation by faith alone through Jesus Christ.

7. The gift of prophecy to our church. It is interesting to note that if you accept the six pillars as remembered by the writer of the list, you have already accepted the seventh, the gift of prophecy, along with the six! It has also been proven true that those who have trouble accepting this gift today are the ones having trouble with the other pillars of our faith. And the ones having trouble with the six pillars of our faith are also having trouble accepting the pillar of the gift of inspiration to our church. The seven pillars all stand together.

But in considering the pillars of our faith, we also need to realize that if we're having problems accepting the spirit of prophecy as evidenced in the days of our pioneers, we will also have problems, in the end, accepting the spirit of prophecy as evidenced in Bible times. What you do with one, you will ultimately do with the other. It is impossible to accept one manifestation and reject the other one. It's both, or none at all.

It was noted in the last century that the steps in the downward course of those who left the faith were as follows: First, there was jealousy and dissatisfaction with those at the head of the work. Next came skepticism in regard to the spiritual gifts to the church. Third came doubt in regard to the vital points of our faith, the pillars of the church. Then came doubt concerning the Holy Scriptures. And finally, our source says, came the "downward march to perdition."— *Testimonies,* vol. 5, p. 672.

I don't even want to begin on these five steps away from the faith, do you? I would like to hold on solidly to the great pillars of the Evangelical Christian world and to the pillars that make us unique as Seventh-day Adventists as well.

It is possible to have your name on the books of the remnant church and still not be one of the remnant. But for those who seek Jesus, He is always there. I want to learn to know Him better and to trust Him more, don't you? I want to learn better how weak I am, even though sometimes I think I am strong. I want Him to pull all the rugs out from underneath me and to topple all of my sand castles, so that I won't depend on anything apart from Him, so that I might be totally and constantly surrendered to His grace. Wouldn't you want Him to do the same for you? That's what the whole business is all about—the gospel of salvation by faith alone in Jesus Christ, as portrayed in these pillars of our church.

The Investigative Judgment Pillar

The study of the investigative judgment pillar may sound to some of you like an exceedingly dry topic. But this has been designated as the central pillar, the primary pillar, of our faith and can prove to be an exciting study for us today. One of the signs of the nearness of Christ's coming is the fact that this pillar is being attacked, just as was predicted it would be in the time of the very end.

One of the charges made against this pillar of our faith is that it is not a Bible teaching. Some have said that it was merely an attempt on the part of our pioneers to come up with some explanation to free themselves from the embarrassment of 1844 and the disappointment. But as we investigate the investigative judgment teaching, we discover that not only is it taught in prophecy, but that Jesus Himself, the greatest Teacher who ever lived, preached the investigative judgment.

Let's begin by finding this pillar in the three angels' messages of Revelation 14. Right in the middle of the first angel's message, Revelation 14:7, we read about the judgment. Let's start with verse 6. ''And I saw another angel fly in the midst of heaven, having the everlasting gospel to preach unto them that dwell on the

2—T.P.

earth, and to every nation, and kindred, and tongue, and people, saying with a loud voice, Fear God, and give glory to him, for the hour of his judgment is come." That's our phrase for this pillar. "The hour of his judgment is come." It doesn't say "is coming" or "will come," but "*is* come." It's here. The first angel's message announced the beginning of judgment.

This is rather interesting, because Paul, in his day, talked and taught about "righteousness, temperance, and judgment to come." Acts 24:25. So in his day, the judgment was still a future event. But by the time of the first angel, the hour of judgment had arrived.

This judgment must take place before Jesus comes, for when Jesus comes, His rewards are with Him, to give to everyone according as his works have been. Matthew 16:27. In order to be fair, there would have to have been an investigation of every case *before* the verdict is given. It is an encouraging Bible truth that God investigates our cases before He comes. Because during the time of investigation, according to Scripture, we have a friendly High Priest at the right hand of the Father, who is our Judge. And He knows by experience what it's like to live in this world. One of the most exciting and meaningful truths that came out of the study of the Adventist pioneers is that we have the benefit of the pre-advent judgment and do not have to face the executive judgment without first having had a hearing in the court with our Judge.

How did the pioneers come across this teaching in the last century? You may recall that after William Miller preached the nearness of Christ's coming, 3000 preachers joined him in proclaiming the message. People from all different faiths listened to and accepted the good news. There were Presbyterians, Catholics,

Baptists, Lutherans, Congregationalists, and all the rest. And they looked forward to the coming of Jesus on October 22, 1844.

They waited all day and all evening and until midnight, and Jesus didn't come. In fact, some waited until dawn of the following day. But nothing happened. And the majority of them gave up, called it all a hoax, and many of them turned on God and faith and the Bible and had nothing further to do with them. But there was a nucleus of people who said, We cannot deny what we heard, what we learned from Scripture and from prophecy.

This group began to study to find out where the believers had made their mistake. They were not willing to discredit the closeness of God and the guidance of the Holy Spirit that had been so apparent. They continued to study. They searched. They met in barns. They got down in the hay and prayed and shed their tears in the hay. Sometimes they spent entire nights searching the Scriptures, studying, until finally something became clear.

The mistake they had made was misinterpreting the section in Daniel 7, 8, and 9 which deals with the judgment. They had thought that the sanctuary to be cleansed was either the world or the church and that they could expect Christ to come to cleanse this earthly sanctuary. But they came to realize that the passage referred to the sanctuary in heaven. They learned of the sanctuary in heaven, after which Moses had patterned the earthly sanctuary. And as they studied the services of the earthly sanctuary in that light, they came to realize that the beginning of the pre-advent judgment in heaven was October 22, 1844. They began to study the sanctuary teachings of Hebrews and saw Jesus' work as our High Priest. They began to preach the first angel's message with new fire, because the announcement that God's judgment had come was now relevant, and it was good news.

During the time of this study, there was a young woman in their midst who had a hard time understanding. Her mind was locked. As they studied, compared, and discussed, she couldn't understand any of their arguments. And the brethren knew she couldn't understand. But she was there praying. After they had studied out the various explanations and were at a loss to know which of the positions was correct, the Lord, through this gift to the church, said, This one, among those you have studied out, is the truth.

This pillar of our faith today, the sanctuary and the investigative judgment, is not something that originated in the beliefs of Ellen White. It was simply verified by her gift. The spirit of prophecy acts as a telescope, in a sense. A telescope doesn't create new stars. It simply reveals stars that were already there and makes them clearer. The telescope is not greater than the stars. It is lesser than the stars. But it still is a great tool for us, with our limited vision, to be able to study the stars and see them more clearly.

In London a man by the name of Ballenger, who was holding meetings with some other evangelists, found that it was his turn to preach on the subject of the sanctuary and the investigative judgment. Being an Adventist, he figured he would have to do it. So he made an attempt. But according to his own testimony, he was so discouraged with his efforts that at the end of his presentation he vowed that he would never again preach on the sanctuary and the judgment until he understood what he was trying to preach.

And then he took a position. He said, I am not going to take it from the people who studied it out and have presented it to us. I can get it from the same source they did. I will study my Bible and I will study commentaries and I will find it for myself.

He began to study. He came to his own erroneous conclusions concerning the pre-advent judgment and the sanctuary in heaven. Ultimately he found himself on the outside of this movement looking in.

Why? Could he have been too proud to admit the need of a special gift to verify personal study? Apparently God is not willing for us to bypass His leading of His people in the past, when we demand special revelation on each truth for us individually. God invites us, and requires us, to study for ourselves. But He also has ordained a system of checks and balances to offset the limitations of each individual's understanding.

The special gift to this church is of great value in trying to understand the bigger issues involved in the investigative judgment. It's true that God doesn't need the investigative judgment to inform Him of anything. It is true that He knows those who are His. But the insights from the gift of prophecy of the connection between the affairs of the universe and the great controversy that is going on help us to understand the reasons for the pre-advent judgment.

Now I would like to list fifteen points, or facts, about the pre-advent judgment and invite you to study each of them more fully for yourself.

Fact #1. There *is* a pre-advent judgment. Revelation 22:11, 12 talks about an announcement made from heaven, "He that is unjust, let him be unjust still: and he which is filthy, let him be filthy still: and he that is righteous, let him be righteous still: and he that is holy, let him be holy still. And, behold, I come quickly; and my reward is with me, to give every man according as his work shall be."

If it is true that Jesus has His rewards settled before He comes, then there would have to have been some sort of determination of those rewards before He comes.

Fact #2. Jesus taught the investigative judgment, as we read in Matthew 22:10-14. The king had called a feast, and those who were invited didn't come—they made excuse. So the servants went out and gathered together as many as they found, both bad and good, and the wedding was furnished with guests.

"And when the king came in to see the guests, he saw there a man which had not on a wedding garment: and he saith unto him, Friend, how camest thou in hither not having a wedding garment? And he was speechless. Then said the king to the servants, Bind him hand and foot, and take him away, and cast him into outer darkness; there shall be weeping and gnashing of teeth. For many are called, but few are chosen." Verses 11-14.

The first thing we notice about this passage is that both the good and the bad alike were invited to the wedding feast. We're all invited. Aren't you glad for that? The invitation to the feast is based upon what Jesus has already done for us at the cross. And apparently many people accept the invitation and accept what Jesus has done for them, and the wedding is furnished with guests.

Then you come to the second part. The king came in to see the guests and saw there a man who was not wearing the wedding garment. The king didn't get angry with him; he called him friend. Notice how patient God is, even with those who spurn His gifts. He asks, "Friend, has there been some misunderstanding? Didn't you get the right information? Do you have something to say?" But the man was speechless.

The order was given to bind him and cast him out into outer darkness. And then those interesting words, "Many are called, but few are chosen."

In every pillar of our faith we will discover two threads running through the whole. The first is what God has done for us in giving Jesus to die in our place. The second is what God wants to do for us in transforming our lives.

We see it here. The invitation represents what Jesus has done for us. Our accepting the invitation to the wedding represents our acceptance of His merits in our behalf. Then the truth of what God wants to do in us, in terms of victory and transformation, is represented by the wedding garment, which we must put on.

This passage obviously teaches a pre-advent judgment. When the king comes in to inspect the guests, there is a work of investigation, of examination, of judgment. The wedding feast occurs prior to the coming of the bridegroom (Jesus) to claim His chosen bride (the church). So this investigation and inspection of the wedding garments takes place before the Second Coming, not at the Second Coming.

Notice this statement from *Christ's Object Lessons:* "By the wedding garment in the parable is represented the pure, spotless character which Christ's true followers will possess. . . . This robe, woven in the loom of heaven, has in it not one thread of human devising. . . . By His perfect obedience He has made it possible for every human being to obey God's commandments. When we submit ourselves to Christ, the heart is united with His heart, the will is merged in His will, the mind becomes one with His mind, the thoughts are brought into captivity to Him; we live His life. This is what it means to be clothed with the garment of His righteousness."—Pages 310-312.

Satan's original charge was that the law of God could not be obeyed. When man broke the law of God, Satan rejoiced and added another charge—that man could not be forgiven. He had no idea that God would pay the penalty Himself. But Jesus' life and death proved that sinners could be forgiven and that the law of God can be obeyed, not only by Jesus, but by those who live the life of faith as He did. This twofold message of forgiveness *and* obedience is the heart of the remnant mission during the time of the three angels and the final work of Christ in heaven. Jesus as our High Priest provides forgiveness for sinners *and* power to obey. These two truths are equally necessary. It is extremely important that the last people of God understand this twofold work of Christ. Otherwise it will be impossible for them to fulfill their mission. Justification by faith, God's work for us, and the righteousness of Christ, which includes God's work in us, are the two themes to be presented to a perishing world.

"Satan had claimed that it was impossible for man to obey God's commandments; and in our own strength it is true that we cannot obey them. But Christ came in the form of humanity, and by His perfect obedience He proved that humanity and divinity combined can obey every one of God's precepts.

" 'As many as received Him, to them gave He power to become the sons of God.' John 1:12. . . . When a soul receives Christ, he receives power to live the life of Christ. . . .

". . . The love of God does not lead Him to excuse sin. . . . He will not . . . overlook our defects of character. He expects us to overcome in His name.

"Those who reject the gift of Christ's righteousness are rejecting the attributes of character which would constitute them the sons and daughters of God.

24

They are rejecting that which alone could give them a fitness for a place at the marriage feast."—*Christ's Object Lessons,* pp. 314-317.

Fact #3. God never does anything unless He reveals His secrets unto His servants the prophets. Amos 3:7. So you could expect anything as big as the king's coming in to investigate the guests would be announced ahead of time. That's why the first angel's message includes the proclamation that the hour of God's judgment is come. And of course, we have already noticed how they got involved in studying that around the time of 1844.

Fact #4. If such an announcement was made by the first angel (that the judgment is here) and if God does nothing without revealing His secrets to His servants the prophets, then you would expect to find a prophecy in the Bible dealing with the investigative judgment, wouldn't you? There is. It's the prophecy found in Daniel 7, 8, and 9. Right here I'd like to give a word of caution. One of the current problems that has arisen concerning the subject of the investigative judgment is that some say there's nothing in Daniel 8 to indicate an investigation or cleansing concerning God's people. If you take Daniel 8 all by itself, that's true. But Daniel 7, 8, and 9 must go together, for they cover the same time period. And Daniel 7 definitely includes God's people in the judgment, the investigation, and the cleansing of the sanctuary. Daniel 7 answers to a great extent those who claim that there is no connection between Daniel 8 and Leviticus 16. Those who make this claim are forgetting that Daniel 7, 8, and 9 are a unit.

Fact #5. One purpose of the pre-advent judgment is to distinguish between those who have accepted the invitation and have put on the wedding garment from those who have accepted the invitation but have failed to put on the wedding garment. Revelation 3:5. There is a passage in Matthew 24 that says, "Because iniquity shall abound, the love of many shall wax cold. But he that shall endure unto the end, the same shall be saved." Verses 12, 13. Notice the verse just before: "Many false prophets shall arise, and shall deceive many."

We live in a time when every wind of teaching is blowing, and the love of many is waxing cold. Again we see the picture in Jesus' own parable that there is something more than merely accepting the invitation. There is enduring to the end and putting on the robe of His righteousness.

"When souls are converted their salvation is not yet accomplished. They then have the race to run; the arduous struggle is before them . . . to fight the good *fight of faith*." (Notice what the fight is—it's the fight of faith!) "The battle is lifelong, and must be carried forward with determined energy."—*My Life Today*, p. 131.

Fact #6. There are books in heaven. "He that overcometh, the same shall be clothed in white raiment; and I will not blot out his name out of the book of life, but I will confess his name before my Father, and before his angels." Revelation 3:5. So there are books in heaven.

Some say, "You mean there are books, with covers and pages, like the books we have? What kind of books are they? Deluxe binding, or paperback?"

Let's face it. We tend to look at God in terms of our human language and understanding. But the Bible is very clear that there are records kept in heaven. It calls them books. Some references to this are in Daniel 7:9, 10; 12:1; Revelation 20:11, 12, 15; 21:27; Luke 10:20;

Philippians 4:3. You may want to look them up for yourself.

Perhaps we ought to reevaluate our ideas of what the books are for. May I remind you that the cross still reaches out in every direction to remind us that God is not trying to see how many people He can keep out of heaven, but rather He is trying to see how many He can get into heaven. One of the reasons for the books, or records, is that the devil keeps track of everything he has caused us to do wrong, so he can throw it in the face of Jesus.

And perhaps God looked down and saw the devil, with his motly records, and said, "You want to keep records? All right. I'll show you how to keep records." And God keeps meticulous records, and does it in a way that the devil's mouth is closed forever.

Fact #7. The pre-advent judgment begins with God's people. First Peter 4:17 says that judgment begins at the house of God. The judgment begins with those who have accepted the invitation to the gospel feast. First Timothy 5:24 suggests the same thing, with some men's sins going before into judgment, and some men's sins following after. So there is a sequence in God's order of judgment.

Fact #8. The investigative judgment gives us an even greater assurance and certainty of salvation. Many today who are questioning the investigative judgment are doing so on the basis of the lack of assurance that they think it brings. This is why it appears in some minds to be up for grabs today.

But let me remind you that the investigative judgment is not up for grabs. It is the people who are questioning it who are up for grabs—not the truth. We are not involved in an attempt today, denominationally, to decide what we believe on the investigative judgment.

That was decided a long time ago. Some people say, "Let's wait until it gets settled." But we don't have to wait. It's already settled. It was settled long ago. We don't wait or hesitate to support this pillar. It was the foundation pillar of the advent faith.

But the reason some people are uncomfortable with it today and are so ready to scrap the idea of an investigative judgment is that apparently their understanding of it has done damage to their assurance. I'd like to point out to you that this is a very self-centered approach to the judgment.

The judgment, as announced by the first angel, is a judgment of *God*, primarily. There are far bigger issues at stake in the great controversy than merely my own salvation. We are not to be preoccupied with our own destiny. We are not to sit around and worry whether we will be saved or lost. That's not our business. That's God's department. He has taken care of it already. See *Steps to Christ*, page 72. Therefore our assurance and certainty are not threatened by the truth of the investigative judgment. What matters is whether or not we are on God's side, in terms of relationship and fellowship and communion with Him day by day.

Fact #9. When a person first confesses his sins, the record of his sins is marked pardoned. But his sins are not blotted out until the times of refreshing (Acts 3:19) or, the ancient types, until the Day of Atonement. What we call the investigative judgment is the time when sins that were earlier marked pardoned are blotted out.

Fact #10. The atonement was not completed at the cross. This fact may startle some of you. But it's as true as your Bible. Hear me out carefully. The atonement was not completed at the cross any more than the Day of Atonement was completed when the sacrifice was offered in the courtyard. You study Leviticus 16 and the whole system of the type, and you discover that the Day of Atonement was not completed until the scapegoat was sent away into the wilderness at the end of the day. I'm not quoting from any commentary or from any inspired reference in addition to the Bible. It's very clear in Scripture that although the sacrifice of Jesus at the cross was complete and finished and enough, the *atonement* and all that it includes was not finished at the cross any more than the Day of Atonement services were finished when the sacrifice was made in the courtyard. That is straight Bible.

Fact #11. There is no need to worry about the architecture of Hebrews 9. If you get bogged down in the architecture of the heavenly sanctuary, you are in needless trouble. The different apartments of the heavenly sanctuary represent different phases of Christ's ministry. When Christ moved from the holy place to the most holy place, His ministry changed in a way that was represented by the different apartments of the earthly sanctuary. In 1844, His ministry for us changed.

Fact #12. You don't have to get bogged down in the problem of how blood can defile the sanctuary. Blood is a witness of death, made necessary by the sin of the sinner. Death and sin defile the sanctuary, and it is this defilement that must be cleansed by the blood of Jesus. There is no problem here if you are open enough not to try to make the illustration stand on all fours, and see simply what is symbolized by the blood that defiles—death because of our sin.

Fact #13. The word *cleansed* in Daniel 8:14 (King James Version) is a good word. We don't need to throw out the phrase, "Then shall the sanctuary be cleansed," as used by our pioneers.

The Septuagint uses the Greek word that we translate as *cleansed*, and the choice of these translators is important. These men lived only about three centuries after Daniel. They decided that the word used by Daniel was best expressed by the Greek word meaning *cleansed*. Who would have had a better idea of knowing what Daniel intended to say? These Greek-speaking Jews used the very best word they could think of to keep Daniel's message clear regarding the cleansing of the sanctuary in heaven.

Fact #14. There is hope for every remnant believer today who sometimes feels confused at all the differing views taken by different scholars and commentaries. We have an inspired commentary that was given for the purpose of settling the disagreements among the uninspired commentaries. What do you do when the scholars disagree? Do you have to become a better scholar than the best in order to settle the disagreement in your own mind? No, let me repeat. God has given to our church an inspired commentary to settle the disagreements among the uninspired commentaries. And we can still be thankful for that today.

Fact #15. God has made provision that none of us needs come up short in the time of judgment. He has issued the invitation to the gospel feast. He has provided the wedding garment as a free gift to all who will accept it.

I would like to invite you today to accept not only the invitation, but the robe of righteousness as well. Don't be content with accepting only half of the gospel. There's no reason for you to remain speechless when you come before the king. The invitation is free, the robe is free, and we can all be there. "He that overcometh, the same shall be clothed in white raiment; and I will not blot out his name out of the book of life, but will confess his name before my Father, and before his angels.'' Revelation 3:5.

The Three Angels' Messages Pillar

The book of Revelation is Jesus' own book. The four Gospels—Matthew, Mark, Luke, and John—teach us much about Jesus and His life and death here on this earth. But the only book in all the Bible that starts out with the phrase "the Revelation of Jesus Christ, which God gave unto him" is the book of Revelation. And it has a growing significance for us as we near the end of time. Although some have become frustrated with the symbols, if you are patient and keep studying, you will discover some of the most glorious truths in all of Scripture.

In the fourteenth chapter of Revelation are the messages of the three angels that constitute one of the pillars of the faith. This is the one unique doctrine of our church. There are other people who believe the Sabbath truth and have held on to that truth for years. There are others who believe the same way we do on the condition of man in death. There are others who accept the gift of prophecy, and there are many, many people, of almost every denomination, who believe in the second coming of Christ. Our only unique contribution to the religious world has been the three angels' messages and the connection they made for us with the sanctuary and judgment teaching.

We have been told that "the end is near. . . . One interest will prevail, one subject will swallow up every other." Do you have any idea what subject that is? It is "Christ our righteousness."—*Sons and Daughters of God*, p. 259. Have you ever thought that the three angels' messages were (1) the judgment is come, (2) watch out for Babylon, and (3) beware of the beast? How can you get the righteousness of Christ out of that?

When we study the history of the acceptance and teaching of the three angels' messages by our pioneers, we discover some very challenging statements. We are told, "There are but few, even of those who claim to believe it, that understand the third angel's message, and yet this is the message for this time."—Manuscript 15, 1888. "Not all our ministers who are giving the third angel's message really understand what constitutes that message."—*Testimonies*, vol. 5, p. 715. That's the kind of thing that can keep a preacher awake at night! Wouldn't it be preposterous for a minister to get up and think he was preaching the third angel's message, and not even understand what constitutes that message?

"We talk about the first angel's message and the second angel's message, and we think we have some understanding of the third angel's message. But as long as we are content with a limited knowledge, we shall be disqualified to obtain clearer views of truth."—*Gospel Workers*, p. 251. "The third angel's message must be presented as the only hope for the salvation of a perishing world."—*Evangelism*, p. 196.

For a long time we as a church have studied carefully, verse by verse, the messages of the three angels, comparing history and prophecy, and have come to conclusions regarding the historical and prophetic

33

teachings of this chapter. But there are also many deep spiritual truths as well that perhaps some have overlooked. And it is the spiritual interpretation that brings to light the manner in which this subject can be swallowed up by the subject of Christ our righteousness.

"And I saw another angel fly in the midst of heaven, having the everlasting gospel to preach unto them that dwell on the earth, and to every nation, and kindred, and tongue, and people, saying with a loud voice, Fear God, and give glory to him; for the hour of his judgment is come: and worship him that made heaven, and earth, and the sea, and the fountains of waters." Revelation 14:6, 7.

Let's take this briefly, phrase by phrase, to see the common thread which runs through all of these messages—a warning against self-worship and an invitation to the deeper life of faith.

"Fear God." We don't need to spend much time on this one. God doesn't want us to be afraid of Him, does He? God is the Creator, and we are only creatures. We should respect Him, hold Him in awe, reverence Him. Jesus came to this world to remove our fear of a God who wants to destroy us. Jesus was exactly like God. He said it in John 14:9, "He that hath seen me hath seen the Father." And Jesus was the kind of Person that little children loved to be around. Sinners and harlots and thieves were not afraid to come into His presence. That was what Jesus was like, and is like. And that is what God is like.

"Give glory to him." One of the classic definitions of justification by faith is that "it is the work of God in laying the glory of man in the dust, and doing for man that which it is not in his power to do for himself."— *Testimonies to Ministers*, p. 456. In the days of Jesus, there was a great deal of emphasis on the glory of man.

Some had trumpets blown before them, advertising the fact that they were going to pray. But Jesus reminded them that the glory had departed. Because whenever the glory of man goes to the top, the glory of God goes to the bottom.

The third part of this first angel's message is, "Worship him that made heaven, and earth, and the sea, and the fountains of waters." That's fourth-commandment language, connecting the Sabbath commandment with this angel's message at the very end of time. If we would remember the Sabbath and what the Sabbath is a sign of, perhaps we would learn to worship God more than to worship ourselves. But here is given the invitation to worship Him, because He is the Creator of everything, including us.

If we don't accept the invitation to worship Him, there is only one option left. We will worship ourselves, in one form or another. We live in a world where people are born worshiping themselves. They are born self-centered. That's been our problem all along in our struggles with sin.

It is only as we come to Jesus and surrender our self-worship, surrender our seeking for glory, and learn to give the glory and reverence and worship to God alone, that we will be able to join those people who someday will stand on a sea that looks like glass, and say, "Great and marvellous are thy works, Lord God Almighty; just and true are thy ways, thou King of saints." Revelation 15:3.

Now let's look at the second angel's message for a few moments. "And there followed another angel, saying, Babylon is fallen, is fallen, that great city, because she made all nations drink of the wine of the wrath of her fornication." Revelation 14:8.

Where did the term *Babylon* come from? What is its

35

origin? It was back in Genesis, the Tower of Babel. It was a tower men tried to build from earth to heaven in an attempt to save themselves. They weren't quite sure that God was big enough to keep His promise not to send another flood. That which followed Babel was Babylon, a whole system of self-worship, of people trying to save themselves. That's what Babylon is all about.

Babylon represents false religions. The common denominator to every false religion is the belief that man can, in some way, save himself. It is only the Christian religion that teaches that mankind needs a Saviour. And even in Christianity, the principle has been introduced in many subtle ways that you can save yourself by your own works. The truth of the righteousness of Christ proclaims that we are saved, both in heaven as well as from the power of sin here and now, by the power and merits of Christ alone.

The third angel's message is found in Revelation 14:9-12. "And the third angel followed them, saying with a loud voice, If any man worship the beast and his image, and receive his mark in his forehead, or in his hand, the same shall drink of the wine of the wrath of God, which is poured out without mixture into the cup of his indignation; and he shall be tormented with fire and brimstone in the presence of the holy angels, and in the presence of the Lamb: and the smoke of their torment ascendeth up for ever and ever: and they have no rest day nor night, who worship the beast and his image, and whosoever receiveth the mark of his name. Here is the patience of the saints: here are they that keep the commandments of God, and the faith of Jesus."

Why does the beast get such bad marks in Scripture? Why did Martin Luther thunder against it in his day? Because if there's anything worse than one person worshiping himself, it's two people worshiping themselves. And if there's anything worse than two people worshiping themselves, it's two million people worshiping themselves. And if there's anything worse than that, it's two million people organized into a system of self-worship.

The beast power is the greatest system of organized self-worship that there has ever been. The system that teaches that people can work their way to heaven by forms, rites, and penances is blaspheming God, for it is placing man in God's department. That's the beast.

What is the image to the beast? Notice this comment from the book *The Great Controversy:* "When the leading churches of the United States, uniting upon such points of doctrine as are held by them in common, shall influence the state to enforce their decrees and to sustain their institutions, then Protestant America will have formed an image of the Roman hierarchy, and the infliction of civil penalties upon dissenters will inevitably result." "But in the very act of enforcing a religious duty by secular power, the churches would themselves form an image to the beast."—Pages 445, 449.

So the image to the beast is trying to enforce a religious duty by secular power. What is secular power? It's human power. So the image to the beast is trying to enforce religious duty by human power. Now transfer that to your own life. Have you ever tried, in your life, to enforce a religious duty by human power? How about your resolutions on December 31? Is it possible, even as a member of the remnant church, to still be enforcing religious duties by human power? And thus to be forming an image to the beast? Ponder it.

Now notice that it says that those who worship the beast, and his image, have no rest day or night. But Jesus said, "Come unto me, . . . and I will give you rest." Matthew 11:28. If you have been trying to enforce religious duties by your own human power, you will be tired. You will have no rest day or night. But it doesn't have to be that way. You are invited to come to Jesus, and He will give rest—rest from working on salvation and rest from working on victory over sin. He offers them both to you, and they are available as you come to Him, and continue to come to Him, for fellowship and communion on a daily basis.

The mark of the beast is self-worship. The mark of the beast is salvation by works. The mark of the beast is trying to save yourself—either from your past sins or from your present sinning or from the world of sin—by anything that *you* can do. And the seal of God, which is the opposite of the mark of the beast, is worshiping God, coming to Him, falling on your knees before Him in total dependence upon Him, learning to trust in Him. The mark of the beast is salvation by works; the seal of God is salvation by faith. The symbols go deeper than even the days of worship they represent.

So again we see that the issue in the three angels' messages is a warning against self-worship and an invitation to worship the Creator.

Some people "think they are committing themselves to God, while there is a great deal of self-dependence. There are conscientious souls who trust partly in God, and partly to themselves. They do not look to God, to be kept by His power, but depend upon watchfulness against temptation, and the performance of certain duties for acceptance with Him. There are no victories in this kind of faith. Such persons toil to no purpose, their souls are in continual bondage, and they find no rest until their burdens are laid at the feet of Jesus."—*Selected Messages*, bk. 1, p. 353.

And then you have Revelation 14:12: "Here is the patience of the saints: here are they that keep the commandments of God, and the faith of Jesus." What is a saint? A saint is one who has been set apart for a holy purpose. And that's the same definition for sanctification. So again you are reminded of what God wants to do in us, as well as what He has done for us. In 1 Corinthians 1:2 we are told that those who are in Christ—those who are sanctified and are called to be saints—are those in every place who call upon the name of Jesus Christ. What does it mean to be "in Christ"? It means to be in relationship with Him, in fellowship and communion with Him. If you are in relationship with Him today, if you have set aside time today for fellowship and communication with Him, you are one of the saints, and you are experiencing not only justification, but sanctification as well.

The everlasting gospel is all throughout these three angels' messages. When people hear the message of these angels and stop worshiping themselves, stop trying to save themselves, stop trying to get the glory for themselves, and bow low at the feet of the only One to worship, then they will experience all of the salvation that He offers. Only the person who gives up on himself understands the power of God. The reason many of us do not understand is that we haven't bowed low at the foot of the cross to receive it.

But we need to realize that only in Jesus can we find rest. As we come to Him day by day, and as we determine to keep on coming to Him the best we know how until we see Him face to face, only then will we realize the rest and the deliverance that He has promised.

The Law of God Pillar

How long has it been since you said to God, "O how I love thy law! it is my meditation all the day"? Or shall we get even closer home? How many students have been saying, "Oh, how I love the rules and regulations here at school. They are my meditation all the day"? Or, as you drive along at 55 m.p.h., how many of you have found yourselves saying, "Oh, how I love the traffic laws. They are my meditation all the day"?

We've noticed so far that two themes run throughout the central pillars of our faith. The two themes that are integral to the remnant mission are (1) the work of our High Priest for us—to mediate His sacrifice made at the cross—and (2) the work of our High Priest in us—to give us power to obey. As we look at the law of God pillar, let's notice two texts.

The first is Revelation 14:12, right at the end of the messages of the three angels. "Here is the patience of the saints: here are they that *keep* the commandments of God, and the faith of Jesus." (Emphasis supplied.)

The other text is equally well known, Revelation 12:17, which talks about the devil being angry with the church, so much so that he went to make war with the remnant of her seed, who *keep* the commandments of God and have the testimony of Jesus Christ.

What is the issue concerning the law of God? When the Bible talks about a remnant people at the very close of time who have a mission, what is their mission relative to the law of God? The issue concerning the law of God is whether it can or can't be kept. Revelation 14:12 doesn't say, "Here are they that teach the commandments of God." It doesn't say, "Here are they that believe with many lawmakers that there has never been any improvement on the Ten Commandments." It doesn't say, "Here are they who think the commandments of God are nice." It says, "Here are they that KEEP the commandments of God." (Emphasis supplied.)

So the real question in this pillar is whether or not the grace of God is enough to enable sinners to *keep* the commandments of God. And that's a rather pertinent question for you as a Seventh-day Adventist.

What was the sequence in understanding for the people who became known, doctrinally speaking, as the remnant? You recall that over 3000 preachers before 1844, both in this country and abroad, were preaching the coming of Christ. Then came the great disappointment, and many denounced the whole thing as a fraud. But there were sincere people who refused to be discouraged. As they continued to study, they came upon a truth known as the sanctuary truth, which involved the study of our High Priest and the judgment. In the process, they found themselves traveling through the court into the holy place, and then into the most holy place, where they discovered the ark that had Ten Commandments in it, the law of God. Thus their attention was focused on the law of God as never before. That's the sequence in which the discovery happened—(1) the second coming, (2) the sanctuary, (3) the law of God.

As they studied the law of God more closely, they began to discover truth they hadn't noticed before. One thing they learned was that the law is the foundation of God's government. If the law of God goes down, God goes down. But God is forever, and so is His law.

Any worthwhile government that we have known has always been based to a great extent on the genius of God's government. No government, human or divine, is stronger than its laws. But there is no law that is any stronger than its penalty for breaking it. And no penalty is any stronger than the actual enforcement of that penalty when the law is broken.

God is interested in running a tight ship. Is that going too far for Him? He is interested in the security of the entire universe. So when God saw sin entering His universe, He saw He had a problem on His hands. He knew that He could not overlook sin or esteem it lightly, or the entire universe would be in jeopardy. God knew that He could not just forgive sins. God has never been able to forgive sins. Are you shocked by that? It's true. God has never forgiven sins. If God could have forgiven sins, then Jesus would not have had to die. Isn't that true? If God could have simply overlooked the whole business and said, "It's OK; we'll just forget it happened," then Jesus wouldn't have had to die.

It was because God could not forgive (overlook) sins that Jesus came and died in our place, *suffering the penalty* for sins. That was proof that God's law is eternal and no one can tamper with His law. And God's government is going to be secure forever. Because God *did not* overlook sin and Jesus *did* come and die, He has been freed to forgive sinners ever since. In this sense, *sins* aren't forgiven, but *sinners* can be forgiven because of the cross.

Of course, the Bible talks about sins being forgiven; we'll admit that. "If we confess our sins, he is faithful and just to forgive us our sins, and to cleanse us from all unrighteousness." 1 John 1:9. But the only reason the Bible talks about sins being forgiven is not because they were simply passed over, but because they are placed on Jesus, thus enabling *sinners* to be forgiven. Jesus' death proved forever that God's law could not be changed, that it could not be done away with. The advent pioneers, as they studied the law, began to get a new appreciation of the *cross*, as they saw the significance of the *law*. Then they gained a greater appreciation of the *gospel,* because they saw how closely it too was related to the law of God and how that a person really can't appreciate the gospel unless he appreciates the law of God in its entirety.

As they studied the gospel with new vision, they came to realize the three parts of the good news of salvation—(1) what Jesus has done for us, (2) what Jesus wants to do in us now, and (3) what Jesus wants to do with us when He comes again.

They were reminded that what Jesus has done for us is clearly stated in 1 Corinthians 15:3, "Christ died for our sins according to the scriptures." They were reminded of what Jesus wants to do in us as they read texts like Jude 24, "Unto him that is able to keep you from falling." And they were reminded of what He wants to do with us when He comes again to "receive us unto himself." By texts such as Hebrews 5:9, "And being made perfect, he became the author of eternal salvation unto all them that obey him," they discovered that although our obedience is not the *basis* of our eternal destiny, it is still a *condition* for eternal life and entrance into heaven.

It's easy to get confused as to the difference between "a condition for" and "a basis of." Someone gave me an illustration on that point that I thought explained it rather well. The college where I am pastor hires the professors on the basis of their education, their experience, and their abilities. A professor's acceptance as a faculty member has to do with his qualifications in these areas. However, it is required that all faculty members have a TB test every year or two. The administration apparently doesn't want teachers who would go around coughing TB germs all over the campus. So to successfully pass the TB test becomes a condition for being on the faculty at the college. It isn't the basis of their acceptance at all, but it's still a condition.

Our obedience is never the basis for our being able to pass in the judgment. But our obedience is still a condition. "In order to be prepared for the judgment, it is necessary that man should keep the law of God."—*The Great Controversy*, p. 435. "Not the hearers of the law, . . . but the doers shall be justified." Romans 2:13. Faith is essential in order to keep the law of God, for "without faith it is impossible to please him." Hebrews 11:6.

We are saved in heaven someday and will enjoy the heavenly country solely on the basis of what Jesus has already done for us at the cross. But it just so happens that God is not interested in having people coughing sin germs all over His country, so He has made obedience a condition for entrance there. The obedience is not what takes us into heaven; it is the blood of Jesus that does that. But obedience is still a condition.

Do you remember who claims that God's law cannot be kept? That's Satan's claim, Satan's charge. It always has been, from the very beginning. Some people say, "God knows that we can't keep His law, can't keep His commandments, so Jesus came and did it for us, in our place." But where do you find that in the Bible? It is the legalist who sees obedience as a basis for salvation. It is also the legalist who does away with obedience in order to have assurance of salvation. If your assurance is based on your behavior or lack of behavior in any way, you are still a legalist. Our assurance is based solely on what Jesus has done for us and on accepting His sacrifice in our place. But this assurance also frees us to accept His power to obey, His power to live victoriously for His glory.

The law is a schoolmaster. It condemns us, but for the purpose of bringing us to the foot of the cross. And when we bow low at the foot of the cross to accept God's wonderful pardon, we stand before Him as though we had never even sinned. God's forgiveness is super-forgiveness, and we can stand before God completely free from guilt.

But there's a second thing that the law does. It also condemns my present sinning, my falling and failing. True? So it also becomes my schoolmaster to lead me to the realization that being put right with God, being justified by His grace, involves something more than just a one-time cleansing at the beginning of the Christian life. This law also leads me to the feet of Jesus for promised strength and power to overcome.

Let me give you a few examples from the Bible to show the truth that the law of God can be kept. They dragged a woman to Jesus, and Jesus said to her, "I don't condemn you." There's the pardon and forgiveness. But He didn't stop there. He added, "Go and sin no more." See John 8:3-11. Would Jesus tell her that if it was impossible for her to stop sinning?

You go to 1 John 2:1. "These things write I unto

45

you, that ye sin not." So it's possible to sin not. But, while we're struggling, growing Christians, we sometimes fall and fail. And the second part is there as well, "If any man sin, we have an advocate with the Father, Jesus Christ the righteous."

Paul says in 2 Corinthians 10:4, 5: "For the weapons of our warfare are not carnal, but mighty through God to the pulling down of strong holds; casting down imaginations, and every high thing that exalteth itself against the knowledge of God, and bringing into captivity every thought to the obedience of Christ." Does that sound like obedience is possible?

Let's notice 1 Thessalonians 5:23, 24, which speaks of sanctification: "The very God of peace sanctify you wholly; and I pray God your whole spirit and soul and body be preserved blameless unto the coming of our Lord Jesus Christ. Faithful is he that calleth you, who also will do it." And you remember Jude 24: "Unto him that is able to keep you from falling, and to present you faultless." These are mighty truths that you cannot deny if you know your Bible. Hebrews 8:10 says it is God's purpose that His law be written in our hearts. And Hebrews 11:6 says, "Without faith it is impossible to please him." Would it be safe to reverse it, and say, "With faith, it is possible to please him"? That is in line with Scripture, for verse 5 says, "By faith Enoch was translated that he should not see death; and was not found, because God had translated him: for before his translation he had this testimony, that he pleased God."

Let's look at just one more, Hebrews 13:20, 21. "Now the God of peace, that brought again from the dead our Lord Jesus, that great shepherd of the sheep, through the blood of the everlasting covenant, make you perfect in every good work to do his will, working in you that which is well pleasing in his sight, through Christ Jesus; to whom be glory for ever and ever, Amen." So if you are ever tempted to believe that God's law is impossible to obey, you'd better go to your Bible and check this subject out for yourself.

The law is not simply negative and condemning, either. God's law is not against us; it's for us. Law—in this world, or in heaven—is not bad news; it's good news. Let me illustrate. I am driving my car down a curving and twisting mountain road. From behind me comes a Porsche, which passes me on a curve and almost has a head-on collision with an oncoming car, which is forced into the ditch to avoid him. I continue on my way, and at the bottom of the hill I see him over by the side of the road having a meaningful dialog with the uniformed driver of a black car with white doors. And I say, "Oh, how I love the law!" The law protects those who obey it as well as condemns those who disobey it.

Obedience to the law can never produce righteousness. But righteousness *will* produce obedience. When Jesus comes into your life, He will produce the righteousness, the obedience; but it's not yours, it's His. That's why Paul said, "I am crucified with Christ; nevertheless I live; yet not I, but Christ liveth in me." Galatians 2:20.

The question is not, Can I keep the law for acceptance with Christ? The question is rather, Can Christ, after He has accepted me, give me power to obey His commandments?

The Bible truth is that the last people before Jesus comes are going to be known (1) for their patience. And if some of you are having trouble with obedience and wondering whether you will ever make it, remember that the saints are known for their patience. They are also going to be known (2) because they keep the commandments of God, and the reason they can keep them is that (3) they have the faith of Jesus.

It is not safe to talk about the need for keeping God's law without also reminding people of God's forgiveness. Some may say, "If we talk too much about His love and forgiveness, this will lead people to play loose with God's mercy and will lead to license." But that's not true, because of the truths revealed in four texts.

The first one is Matthew 18:21, 22. "Then came Peter to him, and said, Lord, how often shall my brother sin against me, and I forgive him? till seven times?" And you remember Jesus' answer, "I say not unto thee, Until seven times: but, Until seventy times seven." This doesn't mean to keep count and stop at the end of 490 times. Jesus is saying that God's forgiveness is unlimited and that ours should be so as well.

The second text is Luke 17:3-5. Jesus said, "Take heed to yourselves: If thy brother trespass against thee, rebuke him; and if he repent, forgive him. And if he trespass against thee seven times in a day, and seven times in a day turn again to thee, saying, I repent; thou shalt forgive him. And the apostles said unto the Lord, Increase our faith."

Would Jesus give us instructions to be more forgiving with our brother than God is with us? Of course not. So this is telling us how God forgives us. Even if we fall and fail seven times in a single day, His forgiveness is unending.

But this will never lead to license. The third text, Luke 7:40-43 comes in the context of the feast at Simon's house. You recall that Simon was a Pharisee. He had been healed of leprosy. He was the one who had led Mary into sin. He wanted to pay Jesus back for healing him. So he threw a feast. "Jesus answering said unto him, Simon, I have somewhat to say unto thee. And he saith, Master, say on. There was a certain creditor which had two debtors: the one owed him five hundred pence, and the other fifty. And when they had nothing to pay, he frankly forgave them both. Tell me therefore, which of them will love him most?

"Simon answered and said, I suppose that he, to whom he forgave the most. And he said unto him, Thou hast rightly judged."

Now let's back up. How many times should we forgive? Seventy times seven—unlimited. How many times in a given day? Seven times—apparently still unlimited. Then, the one who is forgiven the most, loves the most.

Add one more text, John 14:15. "If ye love me, ye will keep my commandments."RSV. So we see that he who loves the most, obeys the most.

What's the conclusion? Will the love and mercy of God ever lead us to play loose with God's law? No, it is the very thing that leads us to keep it. He who is forgiven most, loves the most. And he who loves the most is the one who is going to keep God's commandments.

Some people worry about perfection—but perfection is God's department, not ours. The Bible teaches that we can overcome, that God's law can be kept through the mighty grace of Jesus. Let's leave in God's hands the determination how perfect is perfect, and not spend until midnight discussing that one, OK?

Romans 7:1-4 tells of the frustration of being under the condemnation of the law and of the method to be freed from that condemnation. It's in the form of a parable, and perhaps this expansion of the parable of Romans 7 will help you understand more clearly what we're saying here.

Everyone respected Lawrence. In all of his wide cir-

49

cle of acquaintances you could hardly have found one who wouldn't admit that he really had it all together. Christina was sure that their marriage would be one that was made in heaven. She recognized Lawrence's many fine qualities, and she had learned to—well, not exactly *love* him—but she certainly *respected* him highly. She was sure that love would come as they spent more time together.

The day of the wedding arrived. The soft music began to play, and Christina walked up to the altar to make her public commitment to Lawrence. She promised to remain faithful to him until death would them part, and Christina and Lawrence were pronounced husband and wife. (Married to the law—are you with me?)

But even before the honeymoon was over, the problems began. By the time they had moved into their new home it was most apparent that they didn't like the same things at all. Christina became increasingly unhappy with Lawrence. He wasn't the least bit tolerant. His ideas were set in concrete. She soon gave up even trying to argue with him. It wasn't that he forced her to do things his way, but he was just always there, looking at her reproachfully whenever she would try to unbend and be herself. She grew increasingly weary of his constant condemnation. He not only made judgments about her outward behavior, but he judged her inward motives as well.

Christina tried everything to please him. Day after day she would get up, grimly determined that today would be the day that Lawrence would be pleased with her. But while she was taking extra pains to make one thing perfect, she would discover that something else would be neglected. And there were times when all her best efforts ended in total disaster. It seemed that the harder she tried the more mistakes she made.

Sometimes Christina would become so discouraged that she adopted a devil-may-care attitude, and she would go rashly through the day doing exactly as she pleased. She would take an almost fiendish delight in leaving clothes on the floor, dishes in the sink, while she spent time watching movies on TV and eating chocolates and potato chips by the handfuls.

But—apart from weight—the only thing Christina ever gained, no matter what approach she tried, was a growing awareness of how far short she fell of Lawrence's ideals. Always she could feel his eyes upon her, judging, accusing, condemning.

One night, as she lay quietly beside him in bed, she felt that she absolutely could not stand her life the way it was for even one more day. Lawrence, who had seemed so worthy of her respect and honor at their marriage, now seemed ugly and hateful. She could never please him. It was hopeless to try. No way could she measure up, even for one day, much less for the lifetime she had promised.

If only she could be married to someone else. Someone who would approve of her and love her the way she was. But—"till death do us part"—the words reechoed in her mind. Suddenly she had a bright idea! Lawrence was sleeping quietly beside her. If she could somehow manage to—but how? She soon realized it was impossible for her to kill him. She wasn't strong enough.

Then another idea came. She couldn't kill him. But perhaps she could kill herself. What was life worth anyway, if it had to be lived like this? But to her dismay she found that she didn't have the strength to kill herself either. Yet she couldn't go on any longer. If only she could die and then be resurrected to start life over. Oh, if only she could begin again. In utter despair, realizing that there was nothing at all she could do to help herself, she cried out, "God, if anything gets done to save me from this awful mess, You're going to have to do it, and You're going to have to do it all." For the first time in years she felt peace, and she fell asleep.

Christina awakened early the next morning. Lawrence was still there, apparently. Yet everything seemed somehow different. Perhaps the man beside her was Lawrence's twin brother. There were tears in His eyes and beautiful lines on His face that spoke of some sort of struggle He'd been through. There were also scars in His hands that Christina had somehow not noticed before. Instead of rushing out into the kitchen, she began the day by taking time to communicate with Lawrence. She began to realize that here was One with a kind heart, who would love and accept her whether breakfast was perfectly prepared or not. She began to relax, that very day, and even found herself singing as she did her housework and polished the silverware.

As the days went by, Christina spent more time getting to know this Person. He stayed with her all through the day, yet she still could hardly wait for the next opportunity when she could spend time alone with Him, this One who loved her just as she was and accepted her, even while she was making mistakes.

And somehow, the more loved and accepted she felt, the less she worried about her performance, and the fewer mistakes she made. Lawrence's demands just didn't seem so unreasonable, as they had before.

Then one day Christina realized with a start that her whole relationship with Lawrence had *changed*. She *loved* Him. Not only did she find pleasure in pleasing Him, but her tastes and inclinations were changing.

She now was beginning to love the things He loved.

Once she had thought that only if Lawrence died could she find peace. But it was Christina who had died and had been resurrected to walk in newness of life.

The Faith of Jesus Pillar

Revelation 14:12 describes the people who live just before Jesus comes. "Here is the patience of the saints: here are they that keep the commandments of God, and *the faith of Jesus*." (Emphasis supplied.)

What was the faith of Jesus? Perhaps one of the most exciting truths you can ever realize is the fact that Jesus lived His life here on earth in exactly the way we are to live. I used to think that He had an advantage over us. To discover that Jesus had no advantage over us can tear you apart. But it can bring you untold joy and encouragement to understand that we have a great High Priest who lived life as we have to live it. Of course, there were differences. But I would like for you to notice what some of those differences were and how that the differences made no difference!

Once in a while someone says, Was Jesus like Adam before he fell, or was Jesus like Adam after he fell? And the answer to that is Yes! People have spent many fruitless hours arguing and debating the nature of Christ. There are some aspects of the nature of Christ that we may never understand. But the faith that Christ had we can not only understand, but are invited to experience for ourselves. The faith of Jesus is one of the pillars of our church, and that brings us immediately to the question Did Jesus have faith?

Wouldn't someone who was God as well as man be able to live on His own steam? Did Jesus live through dependence upon someone else, which is what faith is all about? The greatest single definition of faith is trust, and trust is never an end in itself. It always demands an object. We trust another thing; we trust another person. So did Jesus have trust? And if so, in what? in whom?

There is no question that Jesus lived His life here in trust and dependence upon Another, and this truth becomes exceedingly meaningful to struggling sinners. As Jesus' constant trust was in His Father, so the faith of Jesus is the faith of one who depends on someone else rather than on himself or on his own power or strength.

Let's examine the evidence for this, beginning with John 5:19, 30, where Jesus said, "Verily [or truly] I say unto you, The Son can do nothing of himself, but what he seeth the Father do: for what things soever he doeth, these also doeth the Son likewise." "I can of mine own self do nothing: as I hear, I judge: and my judgment is just; because I seek not mine own will, but the will of the Father which hath sent me." It's foolish to consider that Jesus was capable of doing nothing. Someone who is God, as well as man, could do plenty. But obviously the point is that Jesus had come to live life as a demonstration of the trusting faith relationship. He not only came to die for us, He came to show us how to live as well, through dependence upon another power. So Jesus is the greatest single example of how to live the Christian life.

Perhaps He said it best in John 14:10, "Believest thou not that I am in the Father, and the Father in me?" What does that mean? Those kind of phrases show up repeatedly in Scripture. I'd like to remind you that it means simply "in relationship." Jesus was saying, "I am in relationship with the Father, and the Father is in relationship with me. We are in communication. We are in fellowship. We are in personal acquaintance." And as a result of that, He says, "The words that I speak unto you I speak not of myself: but the Father that dwelleth in me, he doeth the works." Verse 10. Through His close relationship with His Father, through the medium of the Holy Spirit, the Father was enabled to do the works we see in Jesus' life.

Now obviously God did not bypass Jesus' capacities. Jesus wasn't left lying in the manger or sitting by the lake somewhere, while God did everything. What God did, He did *through* His Son. Jesus said, "It's the Father who dwells in Me who is doing these things." Not only was the Father the power behind the mighty miracles that people wondered at, but also the obedience that Jesus rendered. Jesus even said in Matthew 19:17, "There is none good but one, that is, God." He was saying that the goodness seen in His life was the goodness of the Father who was dwelling in Him in this close relationship. And for that reason, it is said of Jesus, quoted from Psalm 40:8, "I delight to do thy will, O my God: yea, thy law is within my heart." And Hebrews 1:9 says of Jesus, "Thou hast loved righteousness and hated iniquity."

Now right here I would like to ask a question. Did Jesus actually love iniquity, but hate it even though He loved it, because He knew it was against His Father's will? Or did Jesus, honest and for sure, hate iniquity? If Jesus is our example in how to live the life of obedience, this becomes a very crucial question. Some of you may remember Ken McFarland's parable that was printed in the *Insight* of February 7, 1978; it illustrates what I'm trying to say here. It is called "The Good News Fight."

"Halfway through his nightly recital of the world's hangups, Walter Cronkite's benign countenance suddenly disappeared, replaced momentarily by that commercial starring the Mud Puddle Kid.

"Draped across various items of living-room furniture out there in front of the box were the three Watchers.

" 'That poor Kid's mother really has a problem,' Number One observed, as, up on the screen, The Kid stomped gleefully through several large mud puddles. 'She probably had him all ready to go to a party, and now look at him with that yucky mud all over his clothes.'

" 'Oh, but there's Good News!' enthused Number Two excitedly. 'Just watch now,' he added, pointing to the screen, 'and you'll see that his mom is going to take all those dirty clothes and wash them in Mud-B-Gone detergent. That will solve everything.'

" 'If you've watched this commercial before, then you ought to know that that doesn't solve everything,' retorted Number One. 'Just keep watching.'

"They did, and sure enough, The Kid, sporting freshly laundered clothes, charged back outside to the nearest puddle. As he splattered himself with muddy goo, his mom shook her head and sighed as she tried to look thankful for her box of Mud-B-Gone.

" 'There, you see,' Number One continued, 'what good does it do for her to clean her Kid up if he goes right back and jumps in the mud? I'll tell you what the real Good News is. It's when mom can not only clean The Kid up but also take away his desire to play in mud puddles—maybe even make him hate mud.'

"Number Three hadn't said anything so far, but he'd been thinking, and now he was ready with his dime's worth. 'I think both of you may have a point,' he began, 'but even if Mom can clean up The Kid and then make him hate mud puddles, it seems to me that the problem can never be fully solved until someone takes the mud puddles themselves away. To me, that would really be Good News.'

"Well, it pains me to say it, but the three Watchers became so upset with one another over what constituted the Good News, that they stepped out into the street and started throwing mud at one another.

"The last I saw them, they still hadn't figured out that they all three had seen just a part of the Good News—and it takes all three parts to really solve The Kid's problem.

"But, as Walter says, 'That's the way it is.' "

Now the point that I want to lift out of the middle of the parable is that the author of this parable obviously understood the second portion of the Good News, sanctification, to be not only staying out of mud puddles, but also losing the desire for mud, maybe even learning to hate mud.

And so we are faced with this practical question: Did Jesus really hate the mud puddles, or did He simply stay out of the mud puddles because He loved His Father? Consider these quotations. "Every sin, every discord, every defiling lust that transgression had brought, was torture to His Spirit."—*The Desire of Ages,* p. 111. Jesus "hated but one thing in the world, and that was sin. He could not witness a wrong act without pain which it was impossible to disguise."—Page 88. "His nature recoiled from evil."—*Steps to Christ,* pp. 93, 94. Christ "suffered in proportion . . . to His holiness and His hatred of sin. . . . To be surrounded by human beings under the control of Satan was revolting to Him."—*The Desire of Ages*, p. 700.

I would like to take the solid position that Jesus didn't just hate sin because it was against His Father's will. Jesus was repulsed by sin itself.

Although Jesus never sinned and although He was never self-centered, which is the problem of sin with us, He was still tempted. From the cradle to the grave the devil hounded Him and tempted Him in every possible way. But, wait a minute. If even from His childhood Jesus hated sin, and if He loved righteousness, and hated iniquity, then how could He be tempted? Have you ever felt that it's only the attractiveness of sinful things that causes them to be a temptation? I would like to suggest that the devil really had only one temptation that he could try on Jesus—and that was to get Him to separate from His Father and to depend upon Himself in whatever He did.

If we come to the place that was described in "The Good News Fight" where mud puddles are distasteful to us, where we hate the mud and do not desire it or find it attractive, we will still be tempted. Jesus was, even though He hated iniquity with a perfect hatred. The entire front of all of His temptations was not for Him to do something wrong, but for Him to do something right *in His own power, in His own strength,* which would not have failed Him. He was God.

Throughout His life here on earth, He was tempted to use the power that He could have used. But He never used it. He said, "I can of mine own self do nothing." John 5:30. It was part of the plan of salvation for Jesus to live His life in total dependence upon another power instead of His own. This discovery leads us to a question: Can we have the faith that Jesus had?

Is it possible for these people who live just before Jesus comes to keep the commandments of God because they have, and keep, the faith of Jesus? Right in the three angels' messages we have the indication that those who have the faith of Jesus, and who keep it, are also able to keep the commandments. They don't make cheap excuses for it's not being possible. And they become known as overcomers. The word *overcome* shows up repeatedly in that last book of the Bible. Revelation 2:7, 11, 17, 26; 3:5, 12, 21. Let's read the last one. It's a sample, but it gives us a clue as to how it's possible to overcome.

"To him that overcometh will I grant to sit with me in my throne, *even as I also overcame,* and am set down with my Father in his throne." (Emphasis supplied.) Can we have the faith of Jesus? Yes. Can we keep the faith of Jesus? Yes. Can we overcome as Jesus overcame? Yes.

To say that Jesus overcame is an interesting designation. He didn't overcome from a position of defeat— He overcame from a position of victory. And you don't have to be sinning to overcome. Jesus didn't sin, but He did overcome! Sinners can overcome as well, even as He overcame.

Are there differences between Jesus and us? Of course there are. Jesus was God. We will never be. Jesus never sinned. We have. Jesus was never self-centered. We are born that way. Differences? Yes, but even though there are differences, they do not give Jesus an advantage over us in overcoming temptation. Jesus was God, but He did not use His own God-power as an instrument in overcoming temptation. He depended upon His Father. Jesus never sinned and was never self-centered. But who has the greater temptation to live life apart from God, the One who has the power to do it successfully, or the one who doesn't? Who has the greater temptation to rest on his laurels? The One with the laurels, or the one without?

It is true that we will never be as Jesus was. But this does not mean that we cannot overcome as He overcame. This is a very important distinction. We will never be as Jesus was, but we can obey as He obeyed, we can live as He lived, through dependence upon the power from above instead of our own power from within.

Here are just a few lines to support this premise. Jesus exercised no power that is not offered to us.—*The Desire of Ages,* p. 24. Jesus fought life's battle as we must fight it.—Page 49. Not even by a thought did Jesus yield to temptation. So it may be with us.—Page 123. We are to overcome as Jesus did.—*Thoughts From the Mount of Blessing,* p. 17. Jesus' life in you will produce the same character and works as it did in Him.—Page 78. The list could go on and on and on. It's not just a single, isolated line here or there.

We hear the news that it's just about over. And the devil comes to us and clubs us over the head with our failures. "You have to be perfect," he says, "and you're not even close." But instead of bowing at the feet of Jesus and going to Him for the power to overcome and leaving the results with Him, we try to drag *God's standard* down to *our level* of performance. But assurance is not based on a lowered standard of righteousness—assurance is based only on the grace of the Lord Jesus Christ.

However, this understanding brings us to a very practical problem. Perfect obedience doesn't happen overnight. We don't progress from the point of conversion to the point of constant victory in a single step. We were discussing this in prayer meeting one

Wednesday night when a student stood up and made a speech that was quite impressive. I got a tape recording and had my secretary copy it off. This is what he said:

"It seems to me that the problem is that we're talking about an ideal setup, whereby my desire is to do all that God wants me to do, because my relationship with Him is perfect. He is living, and I'm not living anymore. He is living in me, and my efforts are toward this. If that's true, then there is no need for trying hard to do right. I don't know how many of us here are really in the position of totally depending on God for every area of life yet. If we were, then I guess that's where perfection, which we don't like to talk about, would come in. So since none of us is in that position, all of us are finding that we have to put out effort to overcome the sins in our lives, and it's the very fact that we have to put out effort that could put on the little blinker lights telling us that we aren't depending totally on God yet.

"Now that can be a problem, because then people can be more discouraged than ever. They may think that when they find themselves struggling with sin, they are in a worse position yet, because the struggle tells them they are not depending fully on God. And that's why putting out effort is not a thing, in some sense maybe, that's nice to tell us or teach us. But it's beautiful, because it's the only way overcoming sin is going to work.

"In reality, while we're growing, going through this sanctification process, we cannot help but find ourselves putting out effort to get rid of sin, because we are not perfect now. Imperfection is not right, but it's reality. And this part of reality is a problem that maybe some of us have been thinking you haven't stressed.

And in not stressing this, people get nervous. 'Hey! You don't think that exists? I'm telling you, it exists!'

"All I want to say is, in my experience, reality says I have not conquered. I have not yet given my will to God all the time, in every problem that comes up. And when I don't, it never fails but that I have to put forth effort to not do wrong things. But whenever I pray, 'Lord, I want Your way'—and that happens throughout my relationship with Him—whenever that happens, then I say, 'Hey! I want to go His way.' There's no problem trying not to do this or to do that; I wouldn't do anything else but God's will. That's all I have to say."

I liked the speech, including the "heys." It reminds us of the reality that we do not become totally dependent upon God overnight. Therefore, while we are growing toward ultimate Christian maturity, which in its essence is total dependence upon God all the time, we put forth strong efforts at times because we're not depending upon His strength to keep us from wrong. We still love the mud, but we grit our teeth and do our best to keep out of the mud because we love Jesus. This kind of effort is not what brings victory or genuine obedience. But we are accepted by God as strong people who are overcoming outwardly but not inwardly. We are accepted by Him just as much as are the weak people who don't overcome at all. Jesus' blood covers our sins, whether internal or external. But we need to come to realize that this is not God's goal for us, and to turn to Him for repentance. And this repentance will cut short a thousand struggles to fix up the outside while the inside is still unsurrendered.

The only kind of real obedience that there is comes when in obeying Him we are simply carrying out our own impulses. Our thoughts, our feelings, our purposes, our actions come into harmony with His will. God's purpose for us is to lead us to depend upon Him all of the time, so that we will not only stay out of the mud, but we will hate the mud as well.

Now it is extremely important for us to allow for growth to safeguard us against the false doctrine of "holy flesh." Have you heard of the "holy flesh" doctrine? It goes something like this: If we are in relationship with God and we don't allow for the swing back and forth between dependence upon Him and dependence upon ourselves in the growing Christian life, we will reason this way: "I think I have turned my life over to God, yet I still find myself being impatient or lusting or lying or stealing. But if God is living in me, then it must be OK to do these things." The person who thinks that he proceeds from sin to holiness overnight will assume that whatever he finds himself doing, good or bad, must be God doing it in him. And this can lead to the most flagrant violations of God's law, as it did in the last century.

So we must allow for growth. But while we grow, we have to ask, What do we do with the failures in our Christian lives? Please remember that the people who keep the commandments of God and have the faith of Jesus are also known for their patience. God is patient with us as we grow, and we can also be patient with ourselves. This doesn't mean that we excuse our faults or lower God's standard to our level of performance. But it does mean that we do not become discouraged in our relationship with God because we haven't yet learned to depend upon Him all of the time. We realize that the only way it will ever happen is for us to continue our relationship with Him and allow Him to do His work in our lives, just as fast as He can without destroying us.

In the growing Christian life there will be failures. We shall often have to bow at the feet of Jesus because of our shortcomings and mistakes. Read *Steps to Christ*, page 64. But as we grow in grace and in the constancy of our faith in Jesus, we will not be discouraged with Jesus, even though we may often be disappointed in our own performances.

Neither will we be discouraged with our hope of eternal life, for our hope is based upon what Jesus has done for us at the cross. We trust the Saviour, that "he which hath begun a good work in you will perform it until the day of Jesus Christ." Philippians 1:6. We continue our relationship with Him day by day, so that He is invited into our lives on a daily basis, and by beholding Him, we are changed. It doesn't happen overnight. At times it seems almost imperceptible. But it happens. And the faith of Jesus inevitably leads to keeping His commandments, because of the change that has come inside from the love relationship with Him.

In conclusion, may I tell you that if I had been at the cross, if I had been in Caiaphas' judgment hall, if I had been pushed around by evil men and slapped in the face and spit upon, and if all the time I have had residing within me inherently the power of God, I'm afraid I know what I would have done. Aren't you afraid of what you would have done? I would have said, "It's about time these wretches found out who it is they are pushing around!"

But instead, Jesus was led "as a lamb to the slaughter, and as a sheep before her shearers is dumb, so he openeth not his mouth." Isaiah 53:7. And after He had been shoved and pushed and beaten and spit upon and slapped and scorned, all that came from His lips was, "Father, forgive them; for they know not what they do." Luke 23:34.

5—T.P.

"It was a difficult task for the Prince of life to carry out the plan which He had undertaken. . . . He had received honor in the heavenly courts, and was familiar with absolute power. It was as difficult for Him to keep the level of humanity as it is for men to rise above the low level of their depraved natures, and become partakers of the divine nature."—Ellen G. White Comments, *S.D.A. Bible Commentary,* vol. 7, p. 930.

If you think, still, that He might have had an advantage over you, remember that it was as difficult for Him to keep the level of humanity as it is for us to rise above the low level of our depraved natures.

No wonder Paul said, in Hebrews 4:14, 16, we have a great High Priest, who is passed into the heavens. He knows what it is like to live in a world of sin and trouble and temptation, and He stands there today, inviting you to come boldly to the throne of grace, where you can obtain mercy and find grace to help in time of need.

The Sabbath Pillar

I was in love with a beautiful girl, and I thought she liked me too. But I had a problem. The only opportunity for us to be together for some special time was once a week. The first time we made arrangements for this special occasion, I told her that I would arrive at her house just as the sun was setting, and the sky was all beautiful and purple. I thought that would be romantic. And so I came up the front steps at the very moment I had told her ahead of time, anxious to see her, and I knocked on the door.

Her little brother came to the door. "Where's your sister?" I asked.

"Oh," he said, "I think she's in the shower. But you can come in and wait if you want to."

So I sat down and waited. After a while she came through the house headed toward the kitchen. Her hair was all wet and up in curlers. As she went past me she said a quick Hello and then disappeared into the kitchen.

This was rather disappointing. She seemed to be doing something out there in the kitchen with an iron and ironing board, preparing something for the next day. And I heard the oven door open and shut and some pots and pans rattle around.

I began to wonder if she was very anxious to see me after all. But I continued waiting, and after a while some of the other members of her family came in. She came out of the kitchen, introduced us, and said, "Maybe we can sit down and get acquainted."

But her little brother said, "When are we going to eat?" After a bit of discussion they decided we would eat first, so we went to the table and sat down.

After supper someone said, "Now why don't we go into the family room and get acquainted with our guest."

And someone else said, "Do we have to?"

Well I didn't feel too good about that, but we went into the family room anyway and began to talk together. I noticed that several of them were terribly sleepy, including the young woman that I was most interested in. In fact, she was nodding and yawning. Little brother finally went to sleep right while we were talking.

My weekend with this young woman's family was off to a poor start. I guess you can sympathize with me. She apologized and said, "Listen, I had an awful lot to do this week, and I'm sorry I wasn't ready for your coming, but things will be better tomorrow. We've made some special plans." My heart began to pick up, and I began to feel better.

I went to bed with the picture in my mind of us going to some quiet place where we could really communicate and get to know each other better.

The next day it turned out that she had planned for a group of friends to get together and go out into nature. At first I looked forward to it, but then I found out that all of her friends were bringing their motorcycles. We went out in nature all right—but you couldn't even talk above the roar of the engines out there in the forest. Finally noontime came, and we sat down for a picnic lunch. She seemed to be very tired, and as soon as we had finished eating, she and her friends spread their blankets out under the trees and had a siesta. There was no time to talk then. I found myself walking in the woods, all by myself. I love the woods, but I hadn't planned to be alone like this. I spent most of the afternoon walking in the woods, feeling very lonely.

Finally I returned to the group, and they were awake now. As I approached I could hear them talking. I overheard my friend saying to some of them that she could hardly wait until I left, because she had some exciting plans for that evening as soon as I was gone. I left that weekend, sad and disappointed, because, you know, it's terrible to love someone who really doesn't care much about you.

Now I don't know if you've figured out yet that this is a parable, and that we are talking about the Sabbath. But the God of heaven has set aside twenty-four hours each week, in a special sense, for communication and fellowship with His people. This is one of the pillars of our faith as Seventh-day Adventists.

After the disappointment, the advent pioneers discovered the key that unlocked the sanctuary truth. As they studied the sanctuary teaching and the judgment, they were led into the second apartment of the sanctuary and there discovered the law of God, and especially the fourth commandment. And they became champions of the truth that God's law can be obeyed, including the Sabbath.

If a person were to take the position today that God's law cannot be obeyed, he would immediately be in trouble with the sanctuary teaching, because the sanctuary includes a High Priest who has as one of His main functions the power to keep us from transgression. If a person were to take the position that the law of God cannot be obeyed he would be in trouble with the Sabbath pillar. If you can't keep the law of God, you cannot obey the Sabbath either. If the law goes, the messages of the three angels would go, too, because the third angel culminates in the picture of a group of people who keep the commandments of God. Revelation 14:12. And a person who did not believe that God's law could be obeyed would be in collision with the gift of prophecy given to this church. The pillars of our faith are all interrelated.

You find phrases from the fourth commandment even included in the message of the first angel, in Revelation 14:7, "Worship him that made heaven, and earth, and the sea, and the fountains of waters."

We have studied this pillar in Bible doctrines class and in Sabbath School and in baptismal class, right? We have learned that the Sabbath, as we keep it today, is a memorial of Creation, as well as a memorial of the day Jesus rested in the tomb after His sacrifice was finished and the debt had been paid.

We have also learned that while there is an astronomical reason for the year, for the month, and for the day, there is no obvious astronomical reason for the week. Its only known reason for having continued, unbroken, in its cycle since Creation is that the God of heaven has seen fit to protect it to remind us of Him and of His creative power. And people can claim not to believe in God or admit to His existence, but every time an atheist says, "I'll see you next Friday," he is finished, right there, whether he's willing to admit it or not. The Sabbath is the birthday of the world, and God Himself cannot change a birthday. So how foolish it is for man to try to do so.

How did this Sabbath truth come to the attention of

our pioneers in those early days? There were some who believed in the advent movement of 1844 who lived in the area of Washington, New Hampshire. Among these pioneers were those who were too busy getting ready for the Lord to come to pay much attention at first to what a woman named Rachel Oakes was saying. She had come to that area to visit her daughter, and she was a Seventh Day Baptist. She found very little interest among the advent believers there in the subject of the seventh-day Sabbath. They were so engrossed in the preparation for the second coming of Christ, that they didn't have time to listen at first. It's rather ironic, you know. Suppose she had come with a message concerning the truth that adultery was a sin, or lying or stealing or killing. And they had said, "Don't bother us with that right now; we're busy getting ready to meet the Lord." But gradually the message she carried began to have its effect, and a Methodist preacher by the name of Frederick Wheeler, during 1844, responded and took public stand in favor of the seventh-day Sabbath.

Shortly after this, a man named William Farnsworth, who is now buried in the cemetery behind the Washington, New Hampshire, church, followed suit and accepted the seventh-day Sabbath. Then a Baptist preacher named Thomas Preble accepted and began to write concerning it. Interestingly enough, he included in his writings the warning of Daniel 7:25, that there would be a power that would come along and try to change God's law. Please notice that the Sabbath truth was accepted, studied, and written about by Baptists, Methodists, and others. These people were not Seventh-day Adventists.

About that time a ship captain by the name of Joseph Bates read the writings of Thomas Preble. Bates accepted the seventh-day Sabbath and began to write about it himself. And in 1846 James and Ellen White read the writings of Joseph Bates, and they accepted the Sabbath. So we have the roots of this revival of worship on the seventh day in these early advent believers at that time.

It all happened between the years of 1844-46. As they studied the Sabbath, and its relation to the pillars they had already accepted, they saw its place in the first angel's message of Revelation 14:7. They saw that the warning against Babylon in the second angel's message included the warning against a false day of worship, and they saw how God felt about this false day of worship as indicated in the third angel's message. They accepted the strong warning against it and realized that the final test, or sign, of God's people in the end was that they kept His commandments, including the fourth, and had the faith of Jesus. Revelation 14:12.

But in addition to these more usual things that we think of when we think of the Sabbath pillar, let's spend a few minutes considering an area of the Sabbath that perhaps hasn't been talked about quite as much. Of all places, let's begin with Matthew 11:28. Jesus is speaking, "Come unto me, all ye that labour and are heavy laden, and I will give you rest." Take a second look at that verse. If people who are laboring and heavy laden could find rest by coming to Jesus, then why are they laboring and heavy laden? What's the reason? It would have to be that they are not coming to Christ. Because if they did come to Him, they would not be laboring and heavy laden. Isn't that logical to conclude?

This may sound rather elementary, but let's make sure we understand it before we go on, because we are going to build on this idea for a few minutes. People who are laboring and heavy laden could have rest by coming to Jesus. If they do not have rest, it's because they are not coming to Him.

As long as we are in Matthew 11, let's go ahead and read the next two verses as well, "Take my yoke upon you, and learn of me; for I am meek and lowly in heart: and ye shall find rest unto your souls. For my yoke is easy, and my burden is light." We are familiar with the fact that the yoke represents service. So the key points of this passage are that if people would come to Jesus, and keep coming to Him, they would find rest; and that as they enter God's service and learn more of Him, they get to know Him better as they let others know about what they have learned.

Now let's go to Hebrews 4. In the third chapter of Hebrews, Paul has been describing the experience of the children of Israel in their journey to the Promised Land, a place they could not enter because of unbelief. And in talking to the Hebrew people of his day, Paul reminds them that the problem did not begin and end with the children of Israel. He says in verse 4:3, "We which have believed do enter into rest, . . . although the works were finished from the foundation of the world." Then in verse 4 he introduces the Sabbath, "For he spake in a certain place of the seventh day on this wise, And God did rest the seventh day from all his works." Then he talks about some who did not enter in because of unbelief, and in verse 9 he says, "There remaineth therefore a rest to the people of God."

We are familiar with Paul's statement that if we be Christ's then we are "Abraham's seed, and heirs according to the promise." Galatians 3:29. So we can accept that Hebrews 4 is as much for us as for the He-

73

brews, by Paul's own interpretation. Now I'd like to ask you, what is it that causes a person to become one of the people of God? How did you become one of God's people? Isn't it the fact that you have accepted personally what Christ did for you at the cross that makes you one of the people of God?

What about the children of Israel on their way from Egypt to Canaan? Were they people of God? We have pretty good evidence when God said to Pharaoh, "Let my people go." He claimed them as His people. They offered their morning and evening sacrifices. They celebrated on a daily basis the coming of the Lamb of God to take away the sin of the world.

But notice the context of verse 9. Even for the people of God there is still a further rest available, for it says, "There remaineth therefore a rest *to the people of God."* (Emphasis supplied.)

There are three aspects to salvation that the theologians talk about. The study of salvation is called soteriology, and it has always included three parts: (1) justification, (2) sanctification, and (3) glorification. Justification is my title to heaven, sanctification is my fitness for heaven, and glorification is my entrance into heaven. Justification happens when I first come to Jesus, sanctification happens as I continue to stay with Jesus, and glorification happens when I go with Jesus to heaven. Justification is my freedom from the penalty of sin, sanctification is my freedom from the power of sin, and glorification is my freedom from a world of sin. The first is what God does for us, the second is what God does in us, and the third is what God is going to do with us.

Now the person who has accepted what Jesus has done for us at the cross, one who has accepted the "Lamb slain from the foundation of the world" (Revelation 13:8), is one of the people of God. The person who has given up on ever earning his own way or presenting his own merit or his own works for salvation is one of the people of God. But the text in Hebrews 4 says there is still a rest remaining for the people of God.

What is this rest? Paul uses the Sabbath as an illustration of it. And the Sabbath has always been a sign of sanctification. Ezekiel 20:12, 20. So Paul is talking about the rest in the area of sanctification that is still available for the people of God. Let's read Hebrews 4:10. "For he that is entered into his rest, he also hath ceased from his own works, as God did from his." Have you ever pondered what it was that man did the first day after being created? He spent the first full day resting. Could it have been that tiring, just being created? No. God gave man a reminder right from the beginning that the works were already done, and all that was left for man to do was to join God in rest.

Verse 11. "Let us labour therefore to enter into that rest, lest any man fall after the same example of unbelief." Have you ever seen anyone laboring to rest? I suppose it's possible. I may have even done it myself on occasion. But this reminds us of our first text in Matthew 11:28. "Come unto me, all ye that labour and are heavy laden, and I will give you rest."

We noticed that the reason for the lack of rest was that they were not coming to Jesus, and if they would come to Him, they would have rest. Therefore, what would be the labor? The labor would be in coming to Jesus. It would be putting forth the effort necessary to come to Jesus. And as we labor at that, we find rest, and enter into rest.

There are two texts that sum up the whole subject of salvation through faith in Christ. John 15:5, "Without me ye can do nothing." And Philippians 4:13, "I can do all things through Christ." Put the two together. If without Christ we can do nothing, but with Him we can do all things, then the only thing left for us to do is to get with Him. That's all. It's the same as we read in Matthew 11:28, If we come to Him, we will have rest. When Paul talks about laboring to enter into rest, he is talking about *putting forth the effort* to come to Christ day by day. This sounds very simple and elementary. But one of the biggest problems of the people of God is that they overlook this, and expend no time and effort in coming to Jesus day by day, and thus they don't have any rest. That's why there remaineth a rest for the people of God.

Recent surveys taken within our church have shown that only about one out of five church members is spending any time at all day by day in personal study, communion, prayer, and fellowship with the Lord Jesus. This is our biggest problem as a church today. And this is one of the major reasons why there will be so many who leave the ranks at the very end. We are beginning to see it happen even today. And when that takes place, then those of other faiths who have known what it means to have a personal acquaintance with Christ will come in and replace those who have gone. Isn't that true? It's an exciting time, and a scarey time. But we can lift up our heads and rejoice, because our redemption is drawing nigh.

There is something that is going to come clear to God's people just before He comes, and I believe that a part of this is the deeper meaning of the Sabbath. We have noticed that those who worship the beast and his image have no rest day nor night. Why don't they have rest? The answer is that they are not coming to Christ.

The seal of God is more than just a day; it is a symbol of coming to Jesus and finding rest. Which day of worship we choose shows whom we are worshiping, God or ourselves. And at the very end those who understand the significance of the Sabbath rest will have come to the place of rest by coming to Jesus day by day, and by continuing to come to Him, until He has been able to give them all the rest that He has in mind for His people.

When you read the chapter in *Early Writings* entitled "The Shaking," you find the description of a group of people. They are in agony. It describes them as having agonizing cries, pale countenances, deep anxiety, internal struggle, and large drops of perspiration falling from their foreheads. It also gives one further description, which doesn't seem to fit with the rest at all. It says they have strong faith!

But when you study this chapter, you see that the reason for all of their struggle and anxiety and turmoil is that they haven't obtained the victory yet. And when the scene changes and they are sounding forth melodious praises to God and are surrounded with light and glory, it says they have obtained the victory. The rest that remains for the people of God, which they will come to understand by the very end, if not before, is rest that brings victory.

God's people have come to realize that their own merit and work and effort will avail nothing in earning them a place in God's kingdom. They understand that the forgiveness that Jesus offers is free and cannot be won by any amount of struggle on their part; it is only to be accepted. But there is also a rest available for God's people in the second area of salvation, in living the Christian life, in overcoming sins, and in obtaining the victory over our falling and failing. God's people are to obtain this rest as well, before they can enter the Promised Land, the heavenly Canaan.

So in the end, those who understand the deeper meaning of the Sabbath have rest, both from the condemnation of sin and from its power over their lives. But those who worship the beast and its image will have no rest day nor night.

There are those today who believe that it is not only impossible to obtain the victory, but unnecessary as well. Just for example, let's change the issue of loyalty at the very end from the Sabbath to another of the Ten Commandments. Most of you are aware that the beast power at the end is going to try to force the consciences of God's people. Suppose the issue was not the Sabbath, but the eighth commandment instead.

Suppose it was proclaimed that no one could buy or sell, unless he was willing to become a thief. Suppose it was announced that severe civil penalties would be enforced on those who insisted on being honest in terms of respecting the property of others. And suppose the authorities hauled you into court and told you that if you weren't willing to steal, you would be put to death. And they said, "How do you feel about this issue?"

And you say, "I don't believe that stealing is the right thing to do."

And they said, "Are you saying that you are not willing to steal?"

You reply, "Well, actually I don't believe that anyone can keep from stealing."

They say, "I beg your pardon?"

"I don't believe it's possible for human beings to keep from stealing," you say. "When Christ was here, He didn't steal anything, and His honesty covers for mine. It is impossible and unnecessary for me to keep from stealing. In fact, I'm a kleptomaniac myself."

And they dismiss the case against you. You're already on their side!

If you do not believe that it is possible for the law of God to be kept, then you don't believe that the Sabbath can be kept. And if you don't believe the Sabbath can be kept, there's little chance you would ever be willing to die for the truth of the Sabbath, rather than give it up. Why would you die for something, or even be hauled into court for something, that you can't observe anyway?

Why is it that people are going to be faced one of these days with the question of Sabbath keeping? It's because they not only believe God's commandments are holy and that Jesus kept them, but it is also because they believe they can be kept, and are keeping them. The question of obedience or disobedience is going to be a pertinent question right up to the very end. And your stance concerning whether or not you believe God's law can be obeyed is going to have something to do with whether or not you will stand up for the truth of God, including the Sabbath.

In conclusion, if we who are the people of God, who have accepted rest from trying to earn or merit our own salvation and our own forgiveness from sin, would also accept the rest that is offered to God's people and come to Jesus for rest from our struggling to live the Christian life, we would discover the rest that Paul is talking about in Hebrews 4. We would cease from our own works, as God did from His, and we would know a rest that we have often longed for. We would find His rest for our souls and discover, perhaps for the first time, how easy is His yoke and how light is His burden.

He invites us today to enter into rest concerning the hope of getting to heaven. He invites us to rest from the condemnation of our past sins. He invites us to rest from trying to transform our lives and trying to overcome. Then we will someday be able to enter into the land of rest, the Promised Land, because we have accepted His rest in every area of our lives.

The Life in Christ Pillar

Somehow it didn't seem quite right to call the pillar about the state of the dead the "Dead Pillar," so we have chosen to use the positive side and call it the life in Christ pillar. This is one of the distinctive pillars of our faith. If you took just this one pillar, it would limit the number of denominations you could belong to to just a handful; and if you added the Sabbath pillar, that would clinch it—you would have to be a Seventh-day Adventist. Ours is the only Christian denomination that accepts both.

However, it's interesting to remember that our early advent pioneers were very slow to accept this pillar. It was sort of the johnny-come-lately pillar, as far as the six pillars we have studied are concerned. It was the last one to be accepted by the early Adventist believers.

When some of the pioneers began to get interested in the Bible teaching of what happens to man in death, the majority of the rest of the advent leaders became very upset. In fact, they took measures against these voices, for they were afraid that their beliefs would bring the advent message into ill repute. They were all hanging on tenaciously to the old teaching of the immortality of the soul, including eternally burning hell-

81

fire and all the rest of it. It wasn't until the mid-1850s that the first published material on this pillar came out.

Let's turn to Revelation 14 one more time and find this pillar mentioned there. It's in Revelation 14:13, "And I heard a voice from heaven saying unto me, Write, Blessed are the dead which die in the Lord from henceforth: Yea, saith the Spirit, that they may rest from their labours; and their works do follow them."

Now, of course, anyone who is familiar with the three angels' messages is also familiar with the blessed hope of those who accept this pillar, that their loved ones who have died under the faith of the three angels' messages will come forth in the special resurrection. We understand that what we call "death" is no problem for God and that probably the easiest thing He will ever do will be to raise the dead when He returns.

The teaching that the dead are unconscious has become important, increasingly, over the years as we have seen the rise of modern spiritualism. It seems a logical conclusion to many people that if you go to your reward when you die and if your loved ones are still alive somewhere after death, then you may be able to get in touch with them. So for years Seventh-day Adventists have had a burden to make sure that the dead are good and dead. Sometimes we have been so anxious to make sure of the unconscious sleep of the dead that we forget the words of Jesus, "I am the resurrection, and the life: he that believeth on me, though he were dead, yet shall he live: and whosoever liveth and believeth in me shall *never* die." John 11:25, 26. (Emphasis supplied.)

But if you study the book of John, you will find again the glorious truth that real Christians never die. Jesus didn't like the word *death*. He used it reluctantly. You know what He said to His disciples in John 11, "Our friend Lazarus is sleeping." They said, "That's good. He's been sick; he needs the sleep. Let him keep on sleeping." And finally Jesus said in the words they were used to, "Lazarus is dead." Verses 11-14.

What we are calling death here is only sleep. It is not the kind of death which the Bible calls the wages of sin—if it were, then the devil and his angels should have been dead a long time ago, and all of those who have accepted Jesus should still be alive. No, the wages of sin is what the Bible calls the second death.

I'd like to surprise you by referring in our study to 1 Corinthians 15:3, 4. This may not sound like one of the classical texts on the state of the dead, but let's look at it. "For I delivered unto you first of all that which I also received, how that Christ died for our sins according to the scriptures." That's part one, the number one priority belief of Christians everywhere. Now don't miss part two in the next verse. "That he was buried, and that he rose again the third day according to the scriptures." So Jesus is the great symbol, the great example, of the truth of death and resurrection. The truth of justification is represented by His death, and the truth of sanctification is represented by His resurrection. The twofold work of Christ, in forgiveness for sin and in power to overcome sin, is as much a part of this pillar as of any of the rest of them.

Let's look at Romans 6:3. "Know ye not, that so many of us as were baptized into Jesus Christ were baptized into his death." So when a person accepts Jesus and is baptized, his sins are forgiven, he is justified, and he is baptized into Jesus' death.

Now notice 2 Corinthians 5:14. "For the love of Christ constraineth us; because we thus judge, that if one died for all, then were all dead." You recall Paul's talking about this in his own life. He said, "I die daily." 1 Corinthians 15:31. He accepted God's wonderful, justifying grace on a daily basis. The death of Christ represents the death to self of the person who accepts Christ. Justification is represented by Christ's death. One more text, Galatians 2:20, says, "I am crucified with Christ." Not only was Jesus crucified, not only did He die, but we are to be crucified with Him.

So let's nail it down at this point; the Bible premise is that when we talk about the death of Christ and the spiritual death of the sinner, we are talking about justification. With that in mind, we will move on to the second area that we have been studying, the area of sanctification.

Back to Romans 6 again. Paul not only talks about the death of Christ, but now he talks about life, or resurrection. Romans 6:2: "How shall we, that are dead to sin, live any longer therein?" Verses 4-7: "Therefore we are buried with him by baptism into death: that like as Christ was raised up from the dead by the glory of the Father, even so we also should walk in newness of life. For if we have been planted together in the likeness of his death, we shall be also in the likeness of his resurrection: knowing this, that our old man is crucified with him, that the body of sin might be destroyed, that henceforth we should not serve sin, for he that is dead is freed from sin."

Someone told me a story about a strange funeral. A Christian man had died. When his friends came together at his funeral, an enemy also came. This enemy hated the one who had gone to sleep. According to the friend's knowledge, there was no reason for the hatred. It wasn't fair. But he came. And he could not restrain himself. When the moment came that people were passing by the open casket to pay their last respects, this man came too. He stood there in front of the casket, and he really let the dead man have it. He cursed and swore at him, really told him off.

And the people who told me the story said that they watched carefully. But there was no response whatsoever from the man in the casket. He didn't move an eyelash.

"He that is dead is freed from sin." I'm not sure I'm eager to be dead like the man in the story, but I would like to be dead to sin and freed from sin, wouldn't you?

Let's continue in Romans 6 with verses 11 to 13. "Likewise reckon ye also yourselves to be dead indeed unto sin, but alive unto God through Jesus Christ our Lord. Let not sin therefore reign in your mortal body, that ye should obey it in the lusts thereof. Neither yield ye your members as instruments of unrighteousness unto sin: but yield yourselves unto God, as those that are alive from the dead, and your members as instruments of righteousness unto God." So here we see that not only is Jesus' death indicated, in terms of the believer who has died to self and sin, but Jesus' resurrection, Jesus' living again, Jesus' living within is indicated in the life of the believer. It is talking about both what God has done for us and what He wants to do in us.

Let's go on to 1 Peter 2:24, speaking of Jesus, "Who his own self bare our sins in his own body on the tree, that we, being dead to sins, should live unto righteousness: by whose stripes ye were healed." The only reason we can accept His righteousness in a practical, living, active way and know what it means to be obedient and to overcome is His stripes. The only one who can keep his gaze on Jesus, where the power is in Christian living, is the one who knows that his eternal destiny is already settled by the stripes through which we are healed.

Some say, "We need to keep talking about the law so we will realize how sick we are and go to the Great Physician." But let's not forget that when we go to the Great Physician, we go there to get *well*—to be healed. It is by His stripes that we are healed. And this is a very integral part of the message of the remnant people.

We've already noticed the first part of Galatians 2:20, "I am crucified with Christ." But notice the rest of the verse. "Nevertheless I live; yet not I, but Christ liveth in me: and the life which I now live in the flesh I live by the faith of the Son of God, who loved me, and gave himself for me." Because of Jesus' death and resurrection, it is possible for me to die and yet to rise again—and to have Jesus live His life in me.

Now let's go to Romans 8:11-14: "But if the Spirit of him that raised up Jesus from the dead dwell in you, he that raised up Christ from the dead shall also quicken your mortal bodies by his Spirit that dwelleth in you. Therefore, brethren, we are debtors, not to the flesh, to live after the flesh. For if ye live after the flesh, ye shall die: but if ye through the Spirit do mortify the deeds of the body, ye shall live. For as many as are led by the Spirit of God, they are the sons of God." God's Holy Spirit enables us to rise with Jesus and to walk in newness of life.

"You hath he quickened, who were dead in trespasses and sins. But God, who is rich in mercy, for his great love wherewith he loved us, even when we were dead in sins, hath quickened us together with Christ." Ephesians 2:1-5. Notice that Ephesians 2:1-10 talks about sanctification as well as justification. So then, when we read verses 8 and 9, "For by grace are ye saved through faith; and that not of yourselves: it is the gift of God: not of works, lest any man should boast," we have a great biblical clue as to how we can be obedient and overcome.

Commenting on these verses in Ephesians, *The Desire of Ages,* page 320, says, "Satan cannot hold the dead in his grasp when the Son of God bids them live." Ellen White here speaks at first of the literal, physical death. Then she shifts into a spiritual application: "He cannot hold in spiritual death one soul who in faith receives Christ's word of power. God is saying to all who are dead in sin, 'Awake thou that sleepest, and arise from the dead.' Eph. 5:14."

When we talk about the state of the dead, then, let's not talk only about mortuaries and cemeteries and tombstones and dust. That's really only surface talk. To the Christian death in that sense is but a small matter. It is of little moment. Jesus' death was not the end. It looked like the end to some, but it was only the beginning. And the sinner's death to self and sin isn't the end either. Let's not leave in their graves sinners who have accepted Christ, but let's encourage them to rise and walk in newness of life with Jesus.

In the days of Christ, the Pharisees and Sadducees were at each other's throats all the time. The Sadducees did not believe in a resurrection. That is why they were Sad-you-see! The Pharisees did believe in the resurrection. And one of their favorite topics to argue about was whether or not there really was a resurrection. The Sadducees didn't believe very strongly in the power of God. The Pharisees believed in it but didn't think they needed it. They thought they were doing just fine by themselves, on their own. Both were legalists; both were working on their own salvation.

Today in the spiritual sense it is possible to have Sadducees in the church, who believe in the truth of the cross and the atonement for our sins and God's justification, but there they leave the matter. They do not believe in resurrection from the dead spiritually. They do not believe that God has the power to make us overcomers. They do not believe that we can obey the law of God. They do not accept a High Priest who has two functions, one to mediate forgiveness and the other to give us power to keep from transgression.

The modern Pharisee talks a lot about perfection and the nature of Christ. He believes we ourselves have the power to control our behavior, with God's help, of course. He says, "I haven't sinned for three years." And the modern Sadducee says, "I sin a thousand times a day. Perfection is impossible." Both groups become upset with the other, and they go farther and farther apart. But they are both wrong. Truth lies on another plain entirely.

But watch it. The spiritual Pharisees and Sadducees in the church will unite in the end, just as their counterparts did at the time of Christ. Do you remember what it was that united them? They united at the crucifixion of Jesus.

In conclusion, notice 2 Corinthians 1:9, 10. Here Paul says: "But we had the sentence of death in ourselves, that we should not trust in ourselves, but in God which raiseth the dead: who delivered us from so great a death [do you see justification?], and doth deliver [do you see sanctification?]:in whom we trust that he will yet deliver us [do you see glorification?]."

We were born in this world of sin under sentence of death. But we have heard the invitation not to trust in ourselves, but in God, who raises the dead, not only from the grave, if they sleep, but who raises them here and now. He who has delivered us from so great a death, and doth deliver us, will yet deliver us. It's all there. We can be thankful today for the death and resurrection of Christ and for His promise to finish in our lives the work that He has started, to carry it forward to the day of Jesus Christ. He has the wisdom and the love and the power to prepare us for translation, to make us trees of righteousness, the planting of the Lord, that He might be glorified. Consider this parable of the sapling:

Everett frowned as he looked out across the rows of saplings on the tree farm where he worked as a gardener's helper. One of the saplings—right there in the middle of the bunch—was growing crooked. It leaned to one side, and its branches almost touched the ground. The tree farm had a reputation for producing top-quality stuff, and the way this sapling was headed, Everett knew it would never measure up.

If it continued to grow crooked and bent, eventually the gardner would notice it. And he would give orders for it to be uprooted and sent away. That was the policy at the tree farm, and there were reasons for it.

The saplings were planted fairly close together. One crooked plant could influence a lot of others close to it. Then when the gardner came around, he'd have a whole section uprooted.

Another thing to be considered was how limited the space was on the tree farm. The ground occupied by a crooked sapling should be replanted with a good one.

But Everett did hate to see the saplings dug up and carried away. So he decided to do something to prevent it.

Everett was a student type. He had done more reading about trees and growing them than anybody around. So he hurried back to his room and found some of the best descriptions of a perfect sapling that he could find. Then he rushed back to the sapling and stood right in front of it. "Saplings should be straight and their branches evenly distributed," Everett read loudly. Then he looked over the book and added, "That's from *Counsels to Tree Farmers*, page 94."

The sapling just stood there, bent to one side, its branches drooping.

But Everett continued. "Over here on page 351 of the same book it says, 'The branches must not droop or sag, or the tree cannot be classed as a perfect sapling.' "

The sapling didn't twitch a twig.

Everett waved the book at it to get its attention. "I read on page 177 of *Testimonies to Trees and Shrubs* that if a sapling once gets a bad start it can only be helped by decided efforts. You really ought to try harder to stand up straight."

The sapling still didn't move.

Everett, however, didn't give up that easily. Every day for a whole month he stopped by to read some new quotation to the sapling. He read to it of the thrills of being a mature tree, bearing fruit, being climbed, and making shade. He tried to frighten it by vivid accounts of the fires into which uprooted saplings were eventually tossed. But it was all to no avail. Everett finally gave up.

And the sapling bent over a little further, and its branches touched the ground beneath.

John was also a helper in the garden, and one day he happened to notice the crooked sapling. John was more the aggressive type. He looked the sapling over and said to himself, "That sapling is crooked. I am going straight to the gardener and tell. That way I won't be held accountable for the presence of a crooked sapling."

He headed for the gardener's office, but then he

paused. Somehow he felt a little funny about going. He couldn't say exactly why. It was true that the tree farm was only for straight saplings. And *that* sapling *was* crooked—no doubt about it. And John knew what was right. But still he felt uneasy.

Then he had a splendid idea. He would write a letter to the gardener. That would solve everything. He wouldn't have to sign it.

So he wrote an anonymous letter telling the location of the crooked sapling and how bent and deformed it was.

However, the gardener took a dim view of unsigned letters, and when he saw there was no name he just threw it away and never even bothered to read it. And the sapling's branches began to get tangled and trail on the ground.

Richard worked on the same tree farm, and he noticed the crooked sapling. Richard believed in not getting involved. "Live and let live" was his policy. So he did nothing at all. Occasionally some of the other helpers would mention to Richard the condition of the crooked sapling, but he would shrug his shoulders and say, "Don't hassle it, man. Saplings aren't all alike, you know. It's not my business."

And he looked the other way and was thankful he had learned to be tolerant.

And the sapling bent over a little further, and its branches became even more tangled.

Then one day a new worker came to the tree farm. His name was Andy. Andy had spent a lot of time reading the manuals on tree farming, but he also happened to be close friends with the Author of the books he had read.

He understood a lot of the Author's techniques from having watched how He did things. He knew how the

Author had always loved trees. He also knew that some of the loveliest trees in the Author's own orchard were those that had once looked just like so much kindling to everyone else.

In his association over the years, he had absorbed much of the Author's patience in working with the trees. He knew that it takes time for a tree to grow crookedly and that it also takes time for it to be straightened out again. He believed in the Author's philosophy that even if a sapling *never* responded to all that a gardener could do, the only one who could really make a right decision about when to uproot a sapling would be the one who had loved it and worked with it and tried to save it.

He knew that if he tried to change the tree by some drastic method he would not save time—he would only break the branches.

When Andy saw the crooked sapling he was immediately concerned. He went closer to examine it. The months of neglect had taken their toll. The sapling was very bent—and so Andy went to work at once.

He didn't say much. He just started spending a lot of time with the sapling. He dug about its roots; he freed some of the branches from the ground and untangled them. He tied strings from a nearby post to the sapling's crooked trunk to give it extra support.

At first the sapling resisted. Andy didn't try to force his way. He was just always there—bringing extra water or fertilizer, keeping the soil loose, and shifting the direction of the branches. It became a familiar sight to the others in the grove to see Andy with the crooked sapling, gently working with it.

But as the weeks and months went by, almost imperceptibly, there was a change in the sapling. It stood a little straighter and its branches lifted higher and still higher. At last even the strings were removed, and the sapling stood as straight as any in the grove.

And when the sapling was "transplanted," no one even knew it had ever been crooked.

Is *Sola Scriptura* Scriptural?

One day way back at the turn of the century there was a boy who was swallowed up in the crowd at a large gathering of people, meeting in a huge auditorium with a tin roof. The special meeting that day was for the purpose of listening to a particular woman, but the weather was cloudy and looked like rain. Just as the introduction of this little woman who was to speak was made, the rain came down in torrents and made a deafening sound on the tin roof. This boy who was present wondered how in the wide world any speaker could be heard, let alone this little woman. But when she got up and began her talk, he found to his surprise that he could hear every word.

She continued to speak for a period of time, while her son, who was a preacher, sat on the platform and even did a little dozing. After a while the son stood up and said to his mother, "Mother, it's time for you to stop now. You're going to get tired, and you've talked long enough."

She said, "No, we can't do that. We haven't prayed yet. We must pray." So she went to her knees, and the rest of the people joined her. She began to pray by saying, "My Father," and all through the prayer she talked to God in the first person. Then the meeting was over, but for the boy the memory remained. Because he told me about it years later. He said that after the prayer was finished, he couldn't see a dry eye in the large congregation. The one who told me this story is H. M. S. Richards, and the woman was Ellen White.

During the years of the Reformation, there were three major thrusts that the Protestants identified with. The first was the subject of justification by faith alone in Jesus Christ. The second was what they termed "the priesthood of believers," and the third was *"sola scriptura."* We Adventists are probably more familiar with the first of the three today, but there has been among us a rising emphasis on the other two as well in recent times. Some who have resurrected these two slogans of the Reformation have primarily used them to prove, first, that there is no need for church leadership or church organization (the priesthood of believers) and, second, that there is no need or use for the spiritual gifts in the church *(sola scriptura)*.

However, when you study the use that was made of these phrases at the time of the Reformation, you discover that the Reformers meant something entirely different. When they spoke of the priesthood of the believer, they were not downing church leadership and organization. They were saying that every person who comes to God has direct access to Him, through Christ, and does not need to go through the saints, the priests, or some other intermediary. And it is still good news today that our God is not an inaccessible God, but that we have a High Priest who invites us to come boldly to the throne of mercy for the grace and help that we need.

What did the Reformers mean by the phrase *sola scriptura? Sola scriptura* means by Scripture alone.

One dictionary of theology describes it this way. "As the formal principle of Protestantism, it is the doctrine of the complete sufficiency of Holy Scripture which clearly interprets itself under the Spirit of God, and therefore renders superfluous the church's authority and tradition as real norms of Christian belief." In other words, *sola scriptura* says that the Bible alone is enough for doctrine and practice, without the church and its traditions.

Please notice that the Reformers did not mean there would be no manifestation of light outside of Scripture ever again. Even Martin Luther followed his *sola scriptura* campaign phrases with the additions of, "unless there is clear further and tested revelation." But the enemy of truth has figured out how to make his warfare against the spiritual gifts in the church sound more acceptable by misusing the terms of Reformation history.

The phrase *sola scriptura* does not show up in the Bible. However, we can find some roots of that teaching. Matthew 15:9 records a warning of Jesus against teaching for doctrines the commandments of men, which is what Martin Luther was really against. And we could also use Isaiah 8:20, "To the law and to the testimony: if they speak not according to this word, it is because there is no light in them." So although we cannot find chapter and verse to prove that *sola scriptura* is scriptural, we can see the seeds of the idea in God's Word.

The gift of prophecy, however, is very clear on *sola scriptura*, and this presents a bit of irony. If you are going to march under the banner of *sola scriptura* as a way of doing away with the spiritual gift, you are in that very act doing away with one of the main sources of support for the idea of *sola scriptura!*

Notice a few lines from the introduction to the book *The Great Controversy*, pages vii, viii. "In His word, God has committed to men the knowledge necessary for salvation. The Holy Scriptures are to be accepted as an authoritative, infallible revelation of His will. They are the standard of character, the revealer of doctrines, and the test of experience." There is no one more *sola scriptura* than the author of these words. Yet she continues, "The fact that God has revealed His will to men through His word, has not rendered needless the continued presence and guidance of the Holy Spirit. On the contrary, the Spirit was promised by our Saviour, to open the word to His servants to illuminate and apply its teachings. And since it was the Spirit of God that inspired the Bible, it is impossible that the teaching of the Spirit should ever be contrary to that of the word."

"In harmony with the word of God, His Spirit was to continue its work throughout the period of the gospel dispensation. During the ages while the Scriptures of both the Old and the New Testament were being given, the Holy Spirit did not cease to communicate light to individual minds, apart from the revelations to be embodied in the Sacred Canon. . . . After the close of the canon of the Scripture, the Holy Spirit was still to continue its work, to enlighten, warn, and to comfort the children of God."

It's interesting to note, from the same theological dictionary we quoted from earlier, that in the last analysis the doctrine of *sola scriptura* cannot justify the canon of Scripture, which is not to be found in Scripture. There is nothing in Scripture that designates what the Sacred Canon is. If you are going to take a strong position for the canon of Scripture, you will find your support in the gift of prophecy given to this church or from Luther and the other Reformers.

Which brings us to a vital question: What was the reason or purpose for spiritual gifts in the church? Notice especially Ephesians 4:13, 14. "Till we all come in the unity of faith, . . . that we henceforth be no more children, tossed to and fro, and carried about with every wind of doctrine." That's the reason that God in His love gave the spiritual gifts, including the gift of prophecy. Without it we would have no choice but to continue to disagree.

The Holy Spirit has been promised to guide us into all truth. John 16:13. I heard a scholar say recently, "The Bible teaches that the Holy Spirit will guide us into all truth, not that the scholars will guide us into all truth." And I was glad it came from a scholar! But please notice the difference between two concepts of how the gift of prophecy has worked in the church. One, some think that the spiritual gift was used to present truth that no one had studied or seen before, and therefore became extra-Biblical. The other, that the Holy Spirit used this gift to the church to confirm, ratify, and clarify the conclusions that came from serious, prayerful study. There's a vast difference between the two ideas—and the first is not correct. Our pioneers spent hours and days and weeks in careful personal study, in praying together for light. And the Holy Spirit worked through the gift of prophecy to verify and confirm the Bible truth that was brought to light as they did so.

And we can each be thankful for this gift and this method of enlightenment today. We don't have to spend our lives trying to out-scholar the scholars. We don't have to become experts on the Greek and Hebrew and all the rest of it. We can come to God's Word for ourselves, study for ourselves, and seek the Holy

Spirit's direction—not only through the medium of our own minds, but through the gift of prophecy that was given to our church to settle the differences between those who studied as well.

There was a college Sabbath School class discussion on the campus where I am pastor. A group of students had been given a list of questions about the lesson for that week, and a leader had been appointed to lead the discussion. The subject of the lesson that week was predestination.

As the first question was being discussed, one of the students said, "My ninth-grade teacher said this on the subject." And the group leader said, "That's a good thought, thank you."

As the lesson continued, a second person spoke. "I think that . . ." she said, and gave her own opinion of the answer to the question. And the group leader said, "That was very helpful. I'd never thought of it that way before."

A third student said, "In our Sabbath School lesson quarterly, one of our church leaders is quoted as saying this." And the leader said enthusiastically, "That's a terrific idea."

Finally a fourth person ventured to quote a sentence from the book *The Story of Redemption*. At that point the leader reacted unfavorably and said with a frown, "I think we should stick to the Bible, and the Bible only."

It is true that there have been some who have misused the gift to our church, and perhaps the reaction on the part of some young people particularly has been caused by that. But some of the greatest insights in living the Christian life, some of the finest material on the cross and Jesus' acceptance of us, and some of the most helpful material to deal with the crises facing us today are found in this spiritual gift, and we are the losers if we allow the enemy to deprive us of its benefit.

Let's spend some time in a bit of an old-fashioned Bible study as we consider the significance and importance of spiritual gifts to the church. First, let's read 1 Corinthians 12:1, "Now concerning spiritual gifts, brethren, I would not have you ignorant." That's the apostle Paul talking, and God is reminding us through him that He does not want us to be ignorant on this subject. Perhaps some of us have become ignorant simply because of heredity and environment and having grown up believing in this truth but having never really studied it for ourselves.

Ephesians 4:8: "Wherefore he saith, When he ascended up on high, he led captivity captive, and gave gifts unto men." Verse 11 tells what those gifts were—apostles, prophets, evangelists, pastors, and teachers. And verses 12 to 15 tell the purpose of these gifts. "For the perfecting of the saints, for the work of the ministry, for the edifying of the body of Christ: till we all come in the unity of the faith, and of the knowledge of the Son of God, unto a perfect man, unto the measure of the stature of the fulness of Christ: that we henceforth be no more children, tossed to and fro, and carried about with every wind of doctrine, by the sleight of men, and cunning craftiness, whereby they lie in wait to deceive; but speaking the truth in love, may grow up into him in all things, which is the head, even Christ."

Most of us have seen apostles, for apostles are really missionaries, people sent out to spread the gospel to distant lands. Most of us have seen evangelists, pastors, and teachers. But probably most of us have not seen prophets. I have seen some people who thought they were prophets! It was an interesting experience, a little amusing and a little pathetic at the same time. I've seen some people who thought they were prophets "on the inside looking out," if you know what I mean! But how long has it been since you saw a real, honest-to-goodness, live prophet?

"Oh," someone says, "a prophet is anyone who speaks forth God's word." No. If that were the case there might not be much difference between a prophet and a pastor or teacher. A prophet also is one who has dreams or visions, who has special revelations from the Lord, and who is involved in prediction.

Proverbs 29:18 tells us that the prophet is one who sees visions, and where there is no vision, the people perish. First Corinthians 1:7 says that it's God's purpose for those who are waiting for the coming of the Lord, that they come behind in no gift. And of course you are familiar with Joel 2:28, concerning the young men seeing visions, and old men dreams, and the sons and daughters prophesying in the last days.

First Thessalonians 5:19-21 says, "Quench not the spirit. Despise not prophesyings. Prove all things; hold fast that which is good." And 1 John 4:1 adds, "Try the spirits whether they are of God."

Prophets have had their revelations in different ways, and in light of some of today's discussions, it would be well for us to notice Hebrews 1:1 in order to get something straight concerning methodology. "God, who at sundry times and *in diverse manners* spake in times past unto the fathers by the prophets." God spoke in differing ways, not the same way to each one.

There is a great deal of discussion today concerning relationship between the gift of prophecy in the last church and the use of sources. Not long ago, I came home with some of the latest bits of news about

101

sources and some of the charges that had been made, and shared it with my favorite layperson—my wife. When I had finished, she said, "Well, suppose that in the spirit of prophecy they could show that 51 percent was copied from another source? Where did the other 49 percent come from?" And while I was pondering her answer to that, she continued, "And of all that was copied, how much of it was in error?"

Well, it might take a prophet to know what to copy that was truth, might it not? And God has never limited Himself to one or two particular methods of communicating truth through His servants; in fact, He has taken pains to let us know that He works in differing ways, as He chooses.

In Hosea 12:13 we see a reminder that God led Israel out of Egypt by a prophet. "By a prophet the Lord brought Israel out of Egypt, and by a prophet was he preserved." Second Chronicles 20:20 admonishes, "Believe in the Lord your God, so shall ye be established: believe his prophets, so shall ye prosper."

Now I'd like to do a paraphrase and make an application of a story from 2 Kings 6:8-12. You can look it up and compare if you want to see where I'm substituting. But I think this story of a prophet's work back then gives us a clearer understanding of a prophet's function even in our own time.

"Then the devil warred against God's people and took counsel with his fellow devils saying, Such and such a place shall be my camp. This is my strategy. And the spirit of prophecy sent unto the leader of God's people saying, Beware that thou pass not such a place, for thither the devils are come down. And the leader of the people sent to the place where the spirit of prophecy told him and warned him of and saved himself there, not once, or twice. Therefore the heart of the devil was sore troubled for this thing, and he called his fellow devils and said unto them, Will ye not show me which is for the leader of God's people. And one of his devils said, None, our lord the devil, but the spirit of prophecy that is leading God's people tellest the people of God the words which thou speakest in thy bedchamber.''

We could wish that we had the gift of prophecy in a live form today, and perhaps if we prayed for the living testimony to be revived, we would not pray amiss. But before Moses died, he wrote down in books all that was necessary to take the children of Israel through to the Promised Land, and Joshua simply followed his instructions. And there is plenty of evidence that the gift to this church has given us many helpful warnings and encouragements and counsels that will help us on our way to the heavenly Canaan. Are you still appreciating this gift today, or are you letting the doubts and criticism of the gift affect you? It is true today that the appreciation of the gift of prophecy is going to have something to do with prospering His people.

If you do not accept the gift of prophecy, based upon what the Bible has to say about it, then you don't accept the Bible either. If you don't believe in the gift of prophecy, you don't believe in the Bible, for the Bible teaches that the gift of prophecy has been given to the church from God Himself.

''The written testimonies are not to give new light, but to impress vividly upon the heart the truths of inspiration already revealed.''—*Testimonies*, vol. 2, p. 605. The spirit of prophecy has equal inspiration with the Bible and equal authority with the Bible, but it is still a lesser light.

It is lesser because it is tested by the Bible, and the thing that tests is greater than the thing that is tested. It reveals truth, but it does not manufacture truth. This can be illustrated in the way that archaeologists are constantly discovering and uncovering, but they had better not add anything new to what they have found! Perhaps we can see that this same principle applies to the gift of prophecy.

The gift of prophecy is not an authority over the Bible, but it is an authority on the Bible. Some people have trouble with the phrase, evidently coined by F. D. Nichol, "inspired commentary." But if you accept the inspiration of the gift of prophecy and realize the fact that it is also a commentary on the Bible, and then put the two together, you have an inspired commentary. It is true that the author never claimed to be an inspired commentator, but she never claimed to be a prophet either, and that has nothing to do with whether or not it is true.

When we talk about inspiration, we do not believe in verbal inspiration, that every word was inspired. It was the prophet who was inspired and who expressed in human language what God revealed. This is true both for the Bible and for the gift of prophecy. It may be true that both Bible writers and the gift of prophecy have inaccuracies. They are not infallible. But the inaccuracies in no way affected doctrine, reproof, correction, and instruction in righteousness. The inaccuracies were on unimportant details.

The gift of prophecy to our church was never intended to be an authority on history. If you want to know some of the details of the Battle of Bull Run, during the Civil War, there might be better sources to check. The gift of prophecy was never intended to be an authority on secular matters. One person in our parish said that they had managed to obtain a recipe for curing olives that had originated from Elmshaven. And

they concluded that it was "God's way" of curing olives! Not necessarily. The gift of prohecy to our
church was also never intended to be infallible on bio-
graphical sketches or on chronology. You can read
these disclaimers in the recently published *Selected
Messages*, book 3. It is excellent in dealing with the
subject of inspiration and spiritual gifts. Here is one
statement from it that is pertinent today:

"Those who have been preparing the way for the
people to pay no heed to the warnings and reproofs of
the . . . Spirit of God will see that a tide of errors of all
kinds will spring into life. They will claim Scripture
as their evidence, and deceptions of Satan in every
form will prevail."

"But for all who believe that the Lord has spoken
through Sister White, and has given her a message, will
be safe from many delusions that will come in these
last days."

"One thing is certain: Those Seventh-day
Adventists who take their stand under Satan's banner
will first give up their faith in the warnings and reproofs
contained in the Testimonies of God's Spirit."—
Pages 83, 84.

The choice is up to you. There are many people
who are making their choices today. There are some
who have always had reservations and doubts concerning the gift of prophecy, and they are ready to
throw it out very quickly. But one of the greatest evi-
dences of the love of God is the guidance and hope and
comfort and unity that He has given in this gift. It was
not His purpose that we be carried about by every
wind of doctrine and every deception of the enemy.
And if you believe the Bible and the Bible only, then
you believe in this gift. There is no other way.

Building Under Construction*

No one ever expected it to take so long to finish the building. It should have been completed years before. But there had been repeated delays and setbacks, and at times it seemed that the building was even farther from completion than it had been in times past.

The Architect had sent out a blueprint that gave instructions sufficient to complete the building. But some interpreted the blueprint one way, and some another, and others ignored it completely. Finally the builders became so confused that the Architect issued additional instructions, with even more details, hoping that these additional instructions would explain the original blueprint sufficiently so that no one would misunderstand His plans for the building.

At first it seemed the additional instructions were going to do the trick. The builders were encouraged by the further understandings of the Architect's purposes and began building with renewed vigor and unity. The foundation of the building was solidly built, the walls were being erected, and the central section of the building was completed, with several great pillars sustaining the weight of the construction. The

*Reprinted from *Insight*, July 22, 1980, with permission of the author who wishes to remain anonymous.

builders all looked forward eagerly to the time when the work would be finished and the Architect would come as He had promised He would.

But the coming of the Architect was delayed as the builders allowed other interests to crowd in, and long periods of time passed, with the construction of the building almost at a standstill.

Then a message came from those who had been keeping in close contact with the Architect that He would soon be coming, whether *they* finished the building or not. There was war in the country where the building was being constructed, and there was an enemy who desired more than anything else to see the building and all it surroundings completely destroyed. The watchmen, whose responsibility it was to watch for and warn of the enemy's approach, brought reports that conditions indicated that the enemy soon would be strong enough to work his destruction.

The builders were motivated to begin building again in earnest. But before long all was in confusion. Some of the workers felt that the foundation was inadequate to hold the weight of the building. During the time that interest in the building had waned and the work was neglected, some large sections of the foundation had been covered with rubble and debris. Much of the foundation had been lost sight of. And then, when the work had started up again, it was discovered that some of the workers had built walls out in the fields to the right of the building, and not on the foundation at all. Others had built walls out in left field!

Those who understood the necessity of a solid foundation began to urge that the work be directed primarily toward strengthening the foundation. They insisted that when the foundation was completed according to the blueprint, that would be enough.

There was increasing disagreement as to how the building should proceed. There was so much disagreement that at times the construction was halted for long periods while the workers hurled innuendos, insinuations, insults, and even an occasional brick at one another.

Because of the fact that all the workers had equal access to the blueprint, as well as to the additional instructions, and yet those who read them arrived at differing conclusions, there was a growing tendency to question the sources of information. "The Architect Himself said that all that was really essential for us to know was in the original blueprint," some argued. "If we would limit ourselves to the original blueprint and forget the extra details, then we might find it easier to come to an agreement as to how the building should be built." This idea appealed to many of the workers, and they discarded the additional instructions that the Architect had sent and studied only the original blueprint. "It's not that we don't believe that the additional instructions really came from the Architect," they told those who questioned them. "It's just that we feel that the original blueprint has been neglected, and we're trying to remedy the situation."

Then one day a group of workers gathered in the central section of the building, the part of the building that had been completed immediately after the additional instructions had been given. They had hammers and chisels and began chipping away at the main pillar of the building. "We have consulted the blueprint," they said. "The additional instructions gave a mistaken picture of things. These pillars are built wrong. We're going to tear them down and rebuild them." Many of the workers abandoned their other tasks and joined with this group.

But others of the workers were thoroughly alarmed. "If you tear down the central pillars, the building will not stand," they said.

"Don't be so narrow-minded," the chiselers retorted. "We have been told that until the Architect Himself arrives, there will always be new construction going on. We're just doing some new construction, as was predicted."

"But," the second group of workers insisted, "the additional instructions make it extremely plain that you don't tear down the original pillars in order to begin new construction."

"Oh," they retorted, "are you saying that when the additional instructions contradict the blueprint, we should throw out the blueprint?" And they picked up their hammers and chisels and continued their work.

The construction foreman hurriedly called a meeting to stop the tearing down of the pillars before the whole building came crashing to the ground. Some of those at the meeting thought that the chiselers were right, and that they should be allowed to continue their work. Others thought they were completely wrong and should be forced to leave the construction site, never to return. Still others thought that each person should be free to build or tear down according to his own understanding. And many weren't sure it was important one way or the other—the important thing was to watch for the enemy, who was coming anytime now to try to destroy the building. A few urged that there was much more to fear from within than from without, and that no enemy was needed to destroy the building if the workers tore it down themselves. But their voices were lost in the confusion. The debates continued.

What none of them seemed to realize was that the enemy had already come.